M A

■ ▫ ■ ▫ ■

FULVIO TOMIZZA

MATERADA

Translated from the Italian and with

a Foreword by Russell Scott Valentino

NORTHWESTERN UNIVERSITY PRESS

EVANSTON, ILLINOIS

Northwestern University Press
Evanston, Illinois 60208-4210

Originally published in Italian under the title *Materada* in 1960 by
Arnoldo Mondadori Editore. Copyright © 1999 by Fulvio Tomizza.
English translation and foreword copyright © 2000 by
Northwestern University Press. Published 2000 by arrangement with
Laura Levi Tomizza. All rights reserved.

Printed in the United States of America

ISBN 0-8101-1758-4 (CLOTH)
ISBN 0-8101-1759-2 (PAPER)

Library of Congress Cataloging-in-Publication Data

Tomizza, Fulvio, 1935–
    [Materada. English]
    Materada / Fulvio Tomizza ; translated from the Italian
by Russell Scott Valentino.
        p. cm. — (Writings from an unbound Europe)
    ISBN 0-8101-1758-4 (cloth: alk. paper) — ISBN 0-8101-
1759-2 (paper)
    1. Materada (Croatia) — History — Fiction. I. Valentino,
Russell Scott, 1962–   II. Title.   III. Series.
PQ4880.O4 M313 2000
853'.914—dc21   99-056050

The paper used in this publication meets the minimum requirements of
the American National Standard for Information Sciences—Permanence
of Paper for Printed Library Materials, ANSI z39.48-1984

In memory of my father

■ □ ■ □ ■

CONTENTS

■ □ ■ □ ■

ACKNOWLEDGMENTS

I would like to express my sincere gratitude to the late Fulvio Tomizza for his enthusiastic encouragement, Cinzia Sartini Blum and Maria Esposito for their invaluable linguistic suggestions, and, most of all, Michael Henry Heim for his generous advice, careful editing, and inspirational example.

R.S.V.

■ □ ■ □ ■

FOREWORD

FULVIO TOMIZZA AND THE
WORLD OF *MATERADA*

THE POPULATION ALONG THE ISTRIAN PENINSULA IN THE
northern Adriatic Sea, an area stretching from Trieste to Pula,
has long included a rich ethnic mixture. A Central European
microcosm, Istria has been Roman, Byzantine, Frankish, Vene-
tian, French, Austrian, Italian, Yugoslav, Croatian, and Slovene.
Today it is populated by Croats, Slovenes, Italians, Serbs, Alba-
nians, Montenegrins, Jews, and Germans. The region's recent
history has been dominated by the often tense relations between
Italians and Slavs (Croats and Slovenes).

Immediately following World War II the complex situation
heightened political as well as ethnic issues: in May 1945
Yugoslav partisan forces occupied Trieste; then, in 1947, the
United Nations established the Free Territory of Trieste, dividing it for administrative purposes into Zone A (the city itself)
under the British and Americans and Zone B (an area of two
hundred square miles south of the city) under the Yugoslavs;
finally, in 1954, Zone A was incorporated into Italy, Zone B into
Yugoslavia. In the meantime, Yugoslavia had become a socialist
republic. Unlike the contemporaneous division of Berlin, however, Trieste and its environs was not seen primarily as an ideo-
logical battleground, pitting communist and capitalist forces
against one another. Instead, in traditional Balkan fashion,
international diplomacy considered ethnicity as the key to nor-
malizing relations between the two countries, envisioning the
establishment of "ethnic equilibrium" in border regions.

The cycle of interethnic violence, growing in Istria since the end of the nineteenth century and sorely exacerbated by the anti-Slav policies of Mussolini's rule, far from ceasing with the end of World War II, remained a constant impetus for the ever-growing numbers of the departing. Whether wishing to escape reprisals for atrocities committed before or during the war, fearing the onset of communist rule, or reacting to intimidation and concrete acts of violence against them, political refugees in ever greater numbers streamed across the border. Entire areas of the countryside were abandoned. While the exact number of émigrés has never been accurately established—émigré organizations have tended to inflate, Yugoslavs to deflate the statistics—estimates range from 150,000 to 350,000, beginning in 1945, which in some areas meant as many as 80 percent of the inhabitants. (According to the last reliable census, under the Habsburgs in 1910, the entire population of Istria was under 390,000.)

Tomizza's novel unfolds against the background of the Istrian "exodus," in the spring and summer of 1955 in the northwestern Istrian village of Materada. It chronicles the vicissitudes of the region's farmers in the person of Francesco Koslović, its narrator, who describes the days immediately preceding his family's displacement. Koslović's failed attempts to obtain rights to land that has passed into collective ownership coincide with the departure of an ever greater number of people. Koslović's very name symbolizes the complexity of ethnic relations in the area, and his predicament—whether or not to leave his land, given the increasing encroachment of the *skupčina* (collective) and *društvo* (social league)—represents the main political one.

For Koslović, no clear and exclusive sense of national identity exists. He is a product of the interethnic milieu in which he has lived his life, bilingual and bicultural, both Italian and Croatian, but neither one nor the other exclusively—a transcultured individual. His identity is intimately linked to his surroundings, and he is suggested as the most "natural" outcome of a marginal region which, while undergoing countless changes in regime and shifts in official borderlines, has historically retained its heterogeneous, multiethnic character. In Tomizza's portrayal Koslović is a regional identity with no state representing him. To compound the political and ethnic difficulties, the entire issue is given a personal turn because in Koslović's case a family feud is also involved. His deliberations, often lyrical and nostalgic, and the intense pain with which he faces the notion of departure, provide the connecting thread of the novel's action.

The work is the first novel in Tomizza's *Istrian Trilogy*, the other two being *La ragazza di Petrovia* (*The Girl from Petrovia*, 1963) and *Il bosco di acacie* (*The Acacia Woods*, 1966). These are the first works in a prolific and distinguished career. Tomizza is the author of some twenty novels and the recipient of a host of literary honors, including the prestigious Premio Strega in 1977 for his *La miglior vita* (*A Better Life*) and the Austrian State Prize for European Literature in 1979. His works, moreover, have been translated into more than ten languages, yet to date only one has appeared in English, the somewhat uncharacteristic *Heavenly Supper* (*La finzione di Maria*, 1981).

Materada was a clear departure from previous treatments of the "exodus" in that it portrayed a regional Istrian identity that, far from excluding the area's Slavic roots, showed its dependence on them and emphasized the two elements' coexistence and, indeed, interdependence. It is a portrayal devoid of ethnic hatred. Evil resides in individuals and political institutions, but the goal of ethnicity-based or nationalistic self-definition is rendered practically impossible by the main character's bicultural status. It is replaced by a love for the native region—the tastes, stories, songs, and practices that comprise it now and, most important, comprised it in the past.

The importance of such a treatment should be immediately obvious in the context of twentieth-century Balkan history. Furthermore, the culture of Central Europe, essentially international and interethnic itself—from Kafka to Ivo Andrić to Danilo Kiš—expresses common themes through the filter of a joint historical experience. But this shared cultural conscious-ness exists against a background of great ethnic and religious diversity, a combination that has resulted in countless political and military conflicts, changes of regime, shifts in population. Tomizza's depiction draws its inspiration from a small part of this great diversity, serving to legitimize it against the ravages of nationalist and politically motivated violence. It is an artistic treatment of the tragedy of emigration forced upon those who would have much rather stayed home.

Russell Scott Valentino

■ □ ■ □ ■

MATERADA

THE WAR TRIED US ALL, AS DID THE LIBERATION, WHICH brought its own battles and misfortunes. But it all began for me on one of those pre-Easter days when Uncle Matteo's health had worsened. I was chopping firewood under the oak tree to have everything ready in the house for the holidays and, if need be, the wake—the last paralytic attack had in fact seemed much more serious than the previous ones— when my wife, her face contorted, appeared on the front doorstep and gestured to me to run inside.

Here we go, I thought, and my first reaction was to call my son and send him into Materada and have them sound the church bell. But Oliva grabbed my arm and led me into the dining room, where she closed the door and took a roll of papers from her bosom.

"The thief!" she said, her voice breaking. "Look what he's done, Francesco! Run upstairs quick. Get going!"

I opened the shutters and saw it was my uncle's will, written on a coarse sheet of paper, the ink already faded. Still, it was only too clear. It named his son Carlo as sole heir.

I can't say I was surprised: I had secretly feared as much a thousand times; anything was possible from him. My wife gave me an angry look, narrowing her eyes as if to say her predictions always came true in the end and the fault on every occasion could be no one's but mine. The kerchief holding her hair fell off and, her expression still hard, she didn't pick it up, as if to show she no longer intended to take up her broom and carry on with her chores. I felt something sour in my throat, something clotted scratching the inside, like on windy days when you spread manure or sulfur in the vines. I turned quickly and went into the kitchen and up the stairs that led directly to the old man's room.

He lay in bed, his eyes closed, two fat pillows supporting his head. His breathing was labored, and his face shone with perspiration. It dripped down his forehead and hair, moistening his thick sloping mustache. I moved a little closer to the bed and whispered, "Uncle Matteo."

He slowly opened his eyes, once sky blue now grown dim, no longer shrewd and malignant as when the paralysis came on him or he said he felt sick and then breathed heavily the moment he heard anyone coming up the stairs.

"Uncle Matteo," I said louder, a tremor in my voice. "Uncle Matteo, Uncle Tio. . . ."

He wouldn't make it to the morning, and, God, here I'd worked all my life to give my children a place of their own, to be able to die in my own house with them fully grown and lacking nothing.

"What have you done, Uncle Matteo? The land's mine as much as yours. How could you do a thing like this? How could you stoop so low?"

I had him there beneath me, nailed to the bed, his strength gone, his malice and power emptied into that scrap of yellowed paper. I came closer, my hands nearly above his head, and he still didn't move or make a sign of recognition. And my fate and the fate of my family depended on his life, his recovery.

"Uncle Matteo! Can you hear me?"

I looked down at my long, thick hands; they were useless. And I'd have so liked to do something to him, I didn't know what. I'd have liked to grab hold of him and shake his illness out of him or at least make him suffer a different, healthier pain to take the place of what was killing him, if only until the doctor came. Instead, I left him to his wasted malice and ran downstairs, calling my son, who was somewhere in the haystacks, with all the strength I could muster. I told him to get on his bike right away and ride over to Umago, to his Uncle Berto's, and tell him for the love of God to hurry. I reached to slap him on the back of the head and he dodged me, and I could see he was pleased with himself.

"Should I go for the priest too?"

"No!" I shouted. If you went for the priest, it meant you thought he was as good as dead; I couldn't have cared less if he died afterward, even went to hell! But afterward.

I caught myself in time and added, "Don't bother, Vigi. He'll have gone by then. Quick now!"

My wife was sitting in the kitchen, her head in her hands. My sister-in-law didn't know yet. In fact, she was busy with something at the fireplace and looked at the two of us surprised we were running here and there, crying and screaming as if possessed. Why the surprise? It was painful even when one of the animals died, but nobody in our house was fond of Uncle Matteo, and he'd done nothing to deserve our affection. He'd treated us like servants since we were little. We were always working for him with never a kind word, only orders and rudeness. Besides, he kept everything under lock and key, leaving us barely enough to live on, and only a little extra for Sundays. We put up with him because we were afraid of him: when my brother was still a boy, he had stood up to him a couple of times after seeing him lay hands on our father, his brother, who was as weak and kind as an idiot.

I signaled my wife not to say anything to Maria, but she paid me no heed. There were tears in her eyes.

It was Maria who finally spoke up. "What in the world has got into to you two all of a sudden?" she said chuckling. "Has he started feeling better?" I gave her a dirty look, and she added quickly, "If he's really going to . . . go with God, we'll have to send a telegram to Trieste right away."

Then Carlo would send us another telegram, I thought, telling us to do everything up fine. He might even come and cry at the funeral, not yet knowing he was our new boss. My wife understood it would be better not to say anything to her sister-in-law.

I went outside to listen for the car in the valley below, and it soon grew dark. The hens and turkeys perched on the lowest branch of the oak. All you could hear was a wagon passing slowly over the gravel and a girl coming in from the pasture, singing on her way toward Sterpín. It occurred to me that what with all the clover and new growth in the countryside, the fact that my livestock was closed up in the stalls was a clear sign of mourning.

I went to toss a little hay into their trough, then sat for a long time on the hayloft ladder, staring up at the ceiling, all cobwebs and hay dust. If the old man did die, not even the livestock would be mine—not the cows or steers or the calf that stretched out its neck to lick my hand every time I came near. Uncle Matteo always did everything himself: gathered the harvest, raked in the money, and every once in a while put out a little so we could buy what we needed to carry on the work. "Uncle Matteo," we would say, "the steer's too old. It can't pull anymore. We need a younger one to do the clearing." And the next month the old man (who wasn't a bit old fashioned in this sort of thing: he knew that if you spent money well you came out ahead, and he was an expert at negotiating prices) would bring home a robust young steer with its horns tied. That's the way it was with everything, and because he'd bought everything himself, it all belonged to him, even the clothes I was wearing and the needle and thread my wife sewed with. For some time, actually, Berto and I had been thinking of setting the accounts straight. As long as my father was alive we were content to work and hold our peace, partly out of respect and partly because we believed Father would watch out for us and safeguard the part of the earnings that belonged to us. But he died broke, leaving us only our eyes to cry with, and Uncle Matteo thought he'd done plenty by laying out the money for the funeral. Then the war came and I left for the army, as did my brother. And then came that other misfortune, when the Agrarian Reform took the Kerso lands away, and the old man became even more intractable and ornery than ever.

"You can laugh," he said one night when we were having a good time, joking about something, I don't remember what, "but that was your land." We didn't care; we were even grateful that now our lot was one with his even in adversity. It confirmed in a way that our land was common property and indivisible. Our money, too. We thought he'd put a hefty nest egg away after all those years. But one day in '49 he told us he had only a little over six hundred thousand dinars.

"But how can that be?" my brother asked. "The wheat and grapes alone this year brought in half a million."

"And during the war years?" he countered. "Who thought about your wives and children? I lost a lot during that time. I needed day workers and there weren't any to be had, not even at top prices."

We thought he was just defending himself against accusations of poor management. And in fact he called us into the dining room that very day and explained with the greatest secrecy, "I sent the money to Trieste. There was this sailor I found in Salvore, and we worked out a deal. Times are rough. We can't be sure what's round the corner. We've got to think about putting something over there in a safe place. My son's been saving; he says he'll be able to buy a tavern with it. The Americans left Pola and the people down there had to pack up the little they had and make off. Something like that might happen to us one day. And where can you go when nothing's ready for you? I'll keep track of what's yours from over there, depending on what we get going. If you'd rather not, I can give you what's coming to you next month."

It was true, the times were confused, and the question of Trieste had never been more complicated. De Gasperi wanted the whole of Istria up to the Quieto; the *druzi,* the Yugoslav "comrades," far from giving up, had begun to construct Zone B.

7

"Well," I said, glancing at my brother, "you go ahead, Uncle Tio. We've got enough bread here for now. We can do without the money."

All this was just shrewdness on his part, but it also showed great weakness.

Then in '51 he had a serious heart attack, and we rushed him to the hospital in Isola. By the next day, he had recovered a little, and Berto and I went to visit him. "We don't mean any harm," said Berto, "but you're not getting any younger, and our kids are practically grown up. We've got to think about them, too. The land and the accounts, don't you think it's time to formalize the situation?"

"This isn't the time to talk," was all he said.

And so we came to that Good Friday.

Without realizing it, I'd slipped down from the ladder to the ground and into a pile of hay. I was gripping a handful of it, twisting it in my fury, crunching several strands of it in my teeth. All his lies were running through my head now, everything was becoming clear—even the money for the tavern. It was all just a pretext for him to keep up the swindling. He'd always told us he did everything in our common interest, and in secret he'd dissolved the partnership. Or rather, he knew he was going to die sooner or later and couldn't bear to give up his soul to the devil without performing this last dirty trick. But what hurt me most was that for people like him things always worked out, and regardless of all the socialist talk during the evening meetings at the Center, the Dom, there always had to be someone to take the place of the boss, someone whose shoes were polished, and who went into the fields only on harvest days to pick himself a bunch of grapes, holding it by the stem with two fingers so as not to get his hands dirty, someone very different from those who remembered every handful of manure they'd spread. Fine, the land had gone to the workers with the Liberation, even to people who had squandered it, gambling it away in the taverns and watching it be sold at auction for a song. "The land belongs to those who work it," went the slogan, "to those who have always worked it." And so the Sinkovs had returned to their land, loading their wagon with the wheat Nando had planted and harvested at his own expense (they had even waited for him to harvest it so as not to put themselves out), and when he had rushed out to the field with a guard, demanding payment, they had waved a scythe in his face and whipped his horse, saying that would teach him to think twice before setting foot on other people's land. It was the same with the grapes and corn and alfalfa and olives: they harvested, while he had to pay the taxes, and he couldn't take so much as a vine shoot, because the land appeared as his property at the registry, the parcels were still in his name, like they were when it was Italy, and the officials in Buje didn't go into details. That wasn't what I wanted; that. I asked for what was mine, and that was it. But I wanted it to be my land, recorded in my name at the registry, so I could sell it one day if I felt like it, or give it away, or leave it in my will.

It was Oliva's voice that brought me around and made me aware of the darkness that had filled the stall, the animals' warm breathing.

"Come in," she said, "the doctor's here." Her voice was clear and sure, as if she'd been there all along during my thinking spell. I stood up, and the memory of what had happened just before—the old man's colorless face, the will, her rancor and tears—came upon me like a fit of vomiting.

In an instant I was in Uncle Matteo's room, my shoes still covered with dung, watching the doctor check the old man's blood pressure and heartbeat. He didn't say a word, just did his work, while the old man wheezed. Not being a doctor myself, I thought he was taking too long to find out whether Uncle Matteo would pull through, and I was itching to do something. I waited a little, then made my shoes creak to alert him to my presence. Finally I couldn't stand it any longer. I took two steps forward and asked under my breath, "Doctor, do you think . . . ?"

He turned and signaled to me to be quiet. When at last he covered the sick man, packed his instruments, and went out to the stairs, I took his hand, pressed it tight, and walked him to the kitchen. The women had lit the gas lamp, and I'll never forget it: I didn't even let him come down the last two steps; I blocked his path and said, "Please, Doctor, tell me. . . ."

"Don't worry," he said, smiling, "he'll pull through all right. He's quite strong. He'll come to in a few hours."

I clasped his hand again, and when he saw my glistening eyes, he asked in a kind voice, "Is he your father?"

"No," I said, lowering my head, "my uncle."

After he had washed his hands, Berto gave him a thousand dinars, and he thanked us and left, Maria lighting his way.

I sat down in a chair to rest. To my wife, who was there next to me—I could feel she was calmer, if not altogether relieved—I said in the dark, "Well, tomorrow we can make Easter bread."

"And a dove cake for me," my sneak of a daughter blurted out.

I remembered Uncle Matteo had sold the sheep in January, so this would be the first year for as long as I could remember that we wouldn't have a lamb for Easter.

The eventide bells were ringing. Seeing my son fool with his bicycle pump, I remembered that when Berto and I were his age we were so eager to go play the rattle at the Good Friday service that we would skip dinner. One year we made a rattle as big as a cart. We had so much trouble getting it to Materada that the kids from Cipiani standing in front of the bell tower teased us, asking why we hadn't hitched up the oxen to it. And before the last candle on the triangulum had been snuffed, my brother turned the crank so hard that the priest turned and glared at us.

Many years had passed since then, and we seemed to have entered a new world. The priest was no longer there (he, too, had run off to Trieste), and now it was Gusto Pizze who rang the bells—when he remembered or felt like it.

Maria came back with the light; I forced myself up and called Berto into the dining room to tell him everything. Before going in, I turned to the women and said, "Take him up a bowl of broth."

■ □ ■ □ ■

I I

FORTUNATELY, HE RECOVERED. BUT AS THE WEEK WORE ON he became suspicious of our hushed conversations, and so on the eighth day of the Easter feast he came down to the kitchen, leaning on a cane. We were eating lunch when he appeared at the door. Everyone looked up. He seemed old and tired as he came toward the table. Our silence made him uncomfortable.

He poured himself half a glass of wine and tried to get Nita on his side. "So, did you have your dove cake?"

She must have sensed our worries and our animosity toward Uncle Matteo (after my brother found out about the will, he shook his fist more than once at the ceiling, and one day when we heard a long moan of his, he responded, "Drop dead"), so now she was uneasy, her chin nearly in her plate. Uncle Matteo tried to get his nephew to speak, but a look from Berto made the boy swallow the response.

Everyone was beginning to feel awkward, so I told my daughter, "Didn't you hear what your uncle asked? Go on, answer him."

"Yes, I did."

I tried to put things aright by asking, "How do you feel, Uncle Tio? Do you want a bowl of soup with us? Some meat?"

The women didn't budge.

"No," he said, "I'm not up to that yet. But I'm over the worst, I hope."

My brother snorted, puffed on his cigarette, and made noise with the plates just to make his presence felt.

"Come in, Uncle Tio. We need to talk about something," I said, opening the door to the dining room. It had no furniture but a table and a few chairs. It's in the dining room that we in Istria have meals after weddings and baptisms and bring the deceased when the upstairs rooms are in no condition to be seen by the visitors coming to offer their blessing and, especially, to pry.

Berto came too. I knew it would have been better if he hadn't.

As always in business matters or important things, we spoke *po našu*, that is, in our own language, in Croatian rather than Italian.

"Uncle Tio," I said, "don't you think it's about time we came to some agreement about the land?"

"What do you mean, agreement? Aren't we already in agreement?"

"Yeah," my brother blurted out. "We get to work and you get to collect the profits."

"Slow down, young man."

"Listen to me, Uncle Tio," I said. "You see how weak you've been these last few days. We have to know how things stand. What will be left to us in case of misfortune?"

"Nobody wants to take what's yours."

I felt a great wave of heat run down my spine. I stood up and took the will from the table drawer. "Then what's this?" I asked.

He didn't show the slightest sign of surprise.

"So you've taken advantage of my illness to play this filthy trick on me."

"Excuse me, but the trick you've played on us is much bigger."

"I did notice it was missing from the drawer upstairs. But it's no good anymore. I voided it four months ago."

I caught Berto's eye.

"And now how do you intend to handle things?"

"No one's taking your part from you."

"Thanks so much," said my brother. "That's the second time you've said that. So now tell us how you care to divide things?"

"You've got your land, which, all things considered, is better than mine."

"What land? Valletta? Pizzudo? Salía?"

"Slow down now. Your land is at Kerso. It's more than enough."

Berto and I burst out laughing, but it was a nervous laughter.

"What in hell are you talking about!?"

"Let's be calm. There's nothing to laugh about. You've got forty acres. Even with the woods and the meadow, mine doesn't amount to that much."

"Fine! How do you expect us to take those forty acres? They're under the land reform!?"

"That's another story. I bought the land for you. It's not my fault if the communism came and took it. Go and yell at the communists. I've done my duty."

"What fine words. That's how babies talk. Or morons," said Berto a little too loudly, touching his forehead.

"It's your problem," Uncle Matteo responded in full voice.

"And who always handled the business? Did you ever ask us what we thought?"

He laughed with a sly look in his eyes. "So you knew then that the communism would come." But then he changed his tone and said in a tired voice, "Look, I don't want to fight with you, boys. That land cost me more than sixty thousand lire, and before the war sixty thousand lire really meant something."

I remembered his little deal, the sixty thousand, the "dirty trick," as he himself used to call it. One day in '39, Gelmo, who owned the tavern, invited him to the house. The two of them were big landowners and businessmen and often talked about their dealings. "I've got to close this deal, see," said Gelmo, "a very good deal. The property at Kerso, maybe you've heard, it's been put up for auction. The Rural Bank at Umago is selling it for sixty thousand lire plus a little extra for expenses. It's forty acres of the best land there is around

Materada. Still virgin, hardly used at all, kept as woodland till yesterday practically. What do you think?"

"Sounds pretty good," my uncle must have said, "I'll tell you right off. But this doesn't seem the time to be investing. People are talking about war. Who knows what might happen? Still, they're practically giving it away. When does the sale open?"

"Tomorrow. I've got till noon. All I have to do is show up by eleven-thirty."

The old man went home and was at Umago by dawn. He was back before lunchtime with the news that he'd bought the Kerso property. The very next day I was out there with two steers plowing among the olives. Not until evening, when I went to Giurizzani for tobacco, did I find out about the trick. Gelmo was lying in bed with a fever; his wife didn't even say hello. I cleared things up later with him. I'd had nothing to do with the deal; the old man had done everything on his own. And Gelmo wasn't the type to let himself be seen in a temper, so we were still friends like before. But why, I asked myself now, why hadn't I turned against Uncle Matteo then and there? Why didn't I tell him that wasn't the way honest men behaved, much less friends? I hadn't said a word; I only thought it in my heart (that's the way we are), and the next day I was out there again with the plow amidst those plants that needed only to be covered with a handful of earth in winter to yield olives big as walnuts in autumn.

"Let's not talk like children," my brother repeated. "It's our land, too. You're taking advantage of the fact that Father trusted you blindly and didn't leave a will."

"And what kind of will could he have left?"

"No kind," said Berto, becoming heated, "because your father trusted you blindly too and died without one. He didn't know the kind of man you are."

"Watch yourself, Berto, I'm old enough to be your father twice over."

"So, that's your defense. Your son's in Trieste. Tell me, what's he done to deserve our property?"

"He's my son."

"A chip off the old block."

"Watch what you're saying, I tell you."

"No. You watch what you're doing."

"You're no nephew of mine. You talk like a servant, like a hireling."

"Well, isn't that what we've become? Haven't we always worked under your stick? And when did we once see anything of what was ours? We've always been your hirelings."

The old man tried to get me on his side by flashing me a mean smile that said, "See how petty he is?" But I didn't budge.

"We worked the land," Berto went on. "It's ours. We'll collect everything. You just try and stop us!"

"Those bosses of ours have certainly taught you how to behave."

"Profiteer!" Berto screamed. "You're nothing but a thief!"

The old man's cane fell. He thought Berto had kicked it and bent over to pick it up. But my brother saw the move as the prelude to an attack. He jumped out of his seat and took two steps back, his fists before him. "Just try," he said in a low voice.

I intervened, knocking over a chair in my haste. "Shame on you both! Allowing such things in our house! What would people say?"

I heard the women coming up to the door and Nita crying. I took my brother's arm and told the old man to go outside.

By the time Berto and I came back into the kitchen, he was upstairs in his room. My wife was holding her head in her hands, my sister-in-law was shouting, everyone was on edge. The two little ones started wailing and thcn, who knows why, teasing each other and pulling each other's hair.

I PUT ON MY SUNDAY CLOTHES, AND BERTO AND I WENT DOWN
to the village to see what was going on. We took the Dugazza
road, the prettiest route. Berto stopped to relieve himself at our
old oak, so big that four men couldn't get their arms around it.
Catching up with me, he said, "People like him deserve something bad done to them." There was a tone in his voice I hadn't
heard before.

The road was dry, beautiful, and the starry sky promised
another sunny day. All week we'd been doing odd jobs in the
gardens and around the house so as to have the old man at our
fingertips. We'd planted the tomatoes, squash, sugar beets, and
melons, and now the earth beyond the thick hedges that line our
roads was coming to life, spreading the odor of leaves and grass.

The farms in our part of the country aren't large: farmers
have one field here and another there; they rarely measure
more than two acres or, at most, four and are all surrounded
by hedges or shrubs. Passing through those plots of vines and
wheat and corn and alfalfa, amidst clumps of olive trees, I
recalled all the faces of people—some living, some dead—
who used to meet there with their scythes and plows and barrels on harvest days before the war, when there was poverty
here, yes, but everyone was sure of dying in his own bed.

As we approached Dugazza, I remembered the two youngsters who'd lived in the house there. They were tall and thick
like oaks and had to duck to get through the door. Valentin

had come back from the war with a lung disorder, and every week his brother, Raffaele, assigned others his work in the fields and went to visit his brother at the hospital in Trieste, making the twenty-five-mile journey on foot and in all sorts of weather. In the course of a year he, too, took sick, and his brother kept getting worse. They ended up dying at the same hospital, one month apart, as if they wanted to be close in paradise as well.

The house was terribly old and rickety—you could fit your hand into some of the cracks in the walls—and people kept telling their old mother, who was left all alone there, "You really should leave, Giuditta, or one night we're liable to find you buried under the beams." But she just shook her head. She'd wasted away to nearly nothing, and many people thought she was touched in the head. Finally they took her to Nando's mother-in-law in Giurizzani, Albina, and a few days later we had one of those ugly summer storms, and when it was over there was nothing left but a piece of a wall a few feet high.

"See what's left of Dugazza," said Berto. And I looked at the wall and the mulberry tree where the old lady had kept their goat tied and the stone table where, on hot days, the two young men had their lunch, calling you over for a glass of wine if you happened to pass.

"Yes," I said. "Like two sheaves into a thresher they went. You couldn't say which was better." That was what the war had been for everyone, I said to myself. But then another war had come, all our own, with new deaths and suffering, just when the world was shouting peace and liberation, when the partisans came out of the woods and paraded along the streets of Buje and Umago, hurling their caps into the air, when the new regime took over.

I walked with my head down, staring at the white road, all stones, that led to our tiny capital.

Giurizzani is exactly halfway between Buje and Umago, and all the houses have electric lights. As we came down from Bàbizza, we could hear the commotion from the tavern as far back as the pond—bicycles ringing their bells, young people laughing, a few saxophone and trumpet notes.

"They having a dance?" I asked.

"Easter's over, so they let them," Berto answered.

I was trying to think about other things—it was as if my brother and I had made a pact not to mention Uncle Matteo and the whole ugly business—so as we passed the aqueduct and headed toward the tavern, I listened to the footsteps of the young girls from Cipiani rushing off toward the Dom and the musicians tuning their instruments. Whether or not to let the young people hold a dance had become a serious matter for the new Yugoslav authorities. First, there was the issue of who got the proceeds, which at Giurizzani were always considerable; then, they didn't want to recognize the old celebrations, like the August fairs or other Church feast days, when the receipts were easily double. So the Domestic Affairs Office in Buje had let them have Sundays and the other new holidays like May Day and Tito's birthday. But no celebration was allowed on Easter or Christmas or other feast days. The boys would wander around town and end up drinking at Gelmo's, and the girls would get angry and be in bed by the eventide bells. We understood this was a regime different from any we or our elders had ever seen. They weren't satisfied with making money; they wanted something more. So they left the ballroom dark and people's wallets full on St. Martin's Day, when there was money from the grape harvest, and they put ribbons and colored streetlamps in the Dom on Sundays during Lent or Advent but not during carnival. The first few years it saved money, but that wasn't what made them do it. Then they threw Lent out altogether, and almost overnight the young people got used to the new customs and stopped observing Lent: the priest was no longer around, and they just wanted to kick up their heels. Who could blame them? Now they were running to the Dom from all over, calling to one another by name, whistling and shoving: our band was still considered the best in the district.

We found the usual hubbub at Gelmo's. Sabadin was lying on the bench outside, some stupid kids poking him, giving him more to drink, and telling him his wife was cheating on him with someone from Carsette, or better, with Ciano, the president of the *skupčina*, the collective. Others were bringing their bikes into the shelter, straightening their ties, and unrolling their trousers. There was drinking and singing and card-playing inside, and the room was full of smoke. Gelmo went running from one table to the next, keeping himself busy.

"*Molim lijepo, druzi, izvolite!*"

He had learned these Croatian words (Please, comrades, be my guests) to use with foreigners passing through for a drink; then he had started using them with everyone. I don't know if he was joking or if he really thought there was no one he could trust anymore. In any case, everyone thought him a coward, but sly as a fox, and a schemer. Sure enough, thanks to his scheming, his few words of Croatian, and his talent of worming his way into everyone's good books, he, like few others, had been able to hold on to all his property, without serving a single day in prison or enduring long hours with the interrogators at the Domestic Affairs Office in Buje.

He played on now like an old record player that no longer knows what song's coming out, turning to us at the bar and saying, "*Molim, druzi, izvolite.*"

I gave him a look (the Croatian he spoke was one thing, what we spoke at home was another), and he changed his tune. "Franz, my friend, how are you tonight?" he asked in Italian.

I ordered a beer and watched his sweaty, wrinkled face as he poured it into the glass. That face had clearly gone through quite a bit, though there was some strength left around the eyes. Watching those shrewd eyes, I recalled how my uncle had betrayed his friendship. But I knew that was something he didn't give much weight to, good businessman that he was. It was over and done with and so be it—that's the way such people are: today you win, tomorrow I do. Besides, Gelmo had actually ended up with the last word. My uncle had enjoyed his land for only six years—then the war came, then the collapse, then the Yugoslav occupation, and the land had been given over to the peasants or to owners already weighed down with mortgages and expropriation; and with the money he'd received, Gelmo bought a threshing machine and enlarged the tavern.

So even though I never cared much for his sort and that evening in particular should have cared even less, I felt a certain comfort in his presence. "How's business, Gelmo?" I asked.

"Miserable," he said, pouring something into a funnel and talking as if I were just anybody. "Too many taxes, friend. I can't make it."

"And the farm? Have you tilled the vines or planted your corn? Who's working it for you this year?"

But he was called away to the tables and, holding the beer I had paid for, left without answering.

No, I thought, for him it was all water under the bridge.

Berto went over to one of the tables to watch them play cards and ended up next to Old Man Nin, the best trump and tresette player ever to come from Materada. He didn't play anymore, having deferred to the young, and was now content to watch and lift his cane and rant in his great big voice at the tiniest mistake.

I felt someone nudge my shoulder, turned, and saw it was Milio, who winked at me in his country way. "You here, too, *paesano?*"

"Sure, we came to see the celebration."

"What's up with your uncle? I hear he pulled through."

"Um-hm," I said, "God must be on his side."

"Or the devil," he said, laughing.

But I didn't let him go on. "I hear you've applied. Didn't waste any time."

He felt important then and, taking me by the arm, said, "What can I do? My two little boys can't think of anything else. One wants to join the navy, see the world; the other wants his own profession. Times have changed, Cesco, old pal. Ours was never much of a profession, and young people today don't want to take any risks; they'd rather have a sure paycheck at the end of the week."

The boys from Sferchi were singing at the next table, so we could talk without keeping our eyes peeled. Something had changed recently: the intricate question of Trieste had just then been resolved, for better or worse. A few months before, in November of '54, representatives had signed the London Memorandum, which had Trieste go back to Italy while Zone B passed to Yugoslavia for good. If you didn't feel comfortable staying, you could pick up what little you had and go off to Italy: you could choose to go or not, freely. That appeased our leaders pretty much, and now the guys at the next table could sing a gondolier's song, while in past years heaven forbid anyone should sing in Italian: it was equated with spreading propaganda and had been one of the twenty-four charges against Nando—singing "Santa Lucia" at Gelmo's, though in a way it had been out of defiance toward the guys at another table, who had started in with "*Mi smo pa Istranci, hrvati pravi*" (We are Istrians, true Croatians).

"There's no time to lose. It takes two or three months from the time you apply to when they give permission. By then it'll be summer, and it'll be easier to get settled while the weather's nice. You can even sleep outside if need be the first few days."

"If the summons comes from over there, it means they've arranged to put you up somehow."

"There's a promise. But it's hard to leave the land where your hair's gone gray, leave your home, your people. Would you leave your farm, Franz, where you know every furrow, every blade of grass, every clump of earth?"

A burning sensation came up like a wave from my stomach.

"I'm not leaving anything," I said. "And others will stay too."

"If they only would! I would myself. I've got everything I need. But you just go over to the town hall at Umago some Thursday and look at the line of folks waiting for exit papers."

"Probably people from Umago. It makes sense for them to go. People with nothing but their two hands. Makes no difference carrying bricks and limestone here or in Trieste. Except in Trieste they pay better."

"It's not just people from Umago. They're from Petrovia, Giubba, and San Lorenzo, too. They're all tired. We've been waiting too long. 'Stay home, we'll be back,' the Italian radio used to say, so we stayed put and waited, even if it meant landing in prison or getting beat up, like during the elections."

Milio had been the one to let us in on the goings on in Giurizzani and Cipiani and the other towns in Materada parish. It was April 15, 1950. He had been the first to bring the news—he'd taken the shortcut and climbed up Montecucco—and now he was bragging a little.

"The elections," he said, his ugly features contorting and his eyes flashing. Then everything in his little weasel-like face came ablaze, and he grabbed my arm and started talking breathlessly, chewing up words and curses. "And you want me to stay after I saw them go into houses and destroy everything, slap around men old enough to be their grandfathers, drag around young girls by their hair, shed blood? You want me to stay here with that pack of dogs, with that devil of a Benci, who led them house by house and showed them which ones to smash up, while pretending to be just walking by? With that bottomless pit of a Rozzan, who never gets enough? Look at him, acting all respectable, as if he didn't lead his comrades from the *skupčina* into the Sitars' courtyard. No, I won't stay with that bunch!"

He pointed at old Rozzan, who was watching the cardplayers with his head down. But I stopped him again and said, "Speak softly, friend, you're not on the other shore yet. And anyway, what's got into you all of a sudden? You're all worked up, squeezing my arm like that. And your eyes are all red. You haven't slept for days."

"I keep remembering the elections," he said softly. "It was today, the Sunday after Easter."

Three days before, on Thursday, he had run to our place, white as a sheet, his heart in his mouth. He was trembling, shaking like a leaf. "They're going from house to house with clubs, beating people." Yet terrified as he was, it was clear he was pleased that the Titoists had finally shown their true colors, especially the local ones.

I sat him down, and my brother handed him a glass of wine, but Uncle Matteo yelled over to the women that a small glass of grappa would do more good. He finally calmed down enough to tell us what had happened.

These had been the first elections held in our district since the end of the war and the start of the new regime; they could have determined the fate of the whole area around us: Italy or Yugoslavia. Naturally, there was only one candidate for each office, so by merely going to the ballot boxes you were casting a vote for the new regime. That's why we saw so many unknown faces roaming the towns in those days: men with leather caps, blond, long-haired types, many of whom had been seen fraternizing with our leaders around the Dom. But that morning, Milio said, their numbers had doubled, and they were walking along people's houses, banging hard on the windows, and yelling out in Croatian: "Death to the fascists! Whoever doesn't vote is a fascist! We'll kill all the fascists!"

Toward noon they met old Zorzi from Cipiani on his way home from visiting his brother, Old Man Nin. He took one look at them and started running for home. They caught him easily, beat him up, and left him unconscious in a hedge. Then Benci led them off to Old Man Nin's.

In the courtyard they saw his son Italo, who worked as a waiter at Gelmo's. To raise less of a rumpus, they took him inside, stripped him, and kicked him till he bled, accusing him of having distributed reactionary leaflets. Old Man Nin, twice the size of any of them, lifted his cane, but one of them saw it coming, punched him, and shoved him against the wall. Benci, who up to then had stayed out in the courtyard, ran inside and said, "Enough. What are you doing?" and dragged them back out into the street, where they joined up with the *skupčina* gang.

There were about fifty in all, and they were on their way to Cipiani.

People heard their footsteps and shouts and locked themselves in their houses, taking up a pitchfork here, a scythe there, and waiting. But the men in the street weren't in any hurry; they were happy to take whoever they happened to find, whoever hadn't had time to run. They made do with Luigi Pick, on his way home from the pasture, and let him go only when they saw Lunardo coming at them. Then they broke into groups, only to meet again a short time later under the canopy at the Sitars' place, where they banged on the threshing machine and the tractor, all of them tipsy, partly from the wine they'd drunk to screw up their courage, partly from their rage.

"Who gets the tractor?" they yelled.

"The *skupčina!*"

"Who gets the threshing machine?"

"The *skupčina!*"

"What do the Sitars get?"

"The grave!"

All at once the Sitars' door opened and the youngest of the sons stepped out a few paces onto the gravel. That was all they needed. Before the eyes of the women, who were screaming and threatening to throw themselves from the windows, they grabbed hold of the boy and dragged him like a dead weight into the wheatfield nearby.

He didn't scream, but you could hear people screaming from all the windows and doorways of the other houses. The women, their hair down, their teeth chattering, began burning olive branches, like we do to keep the hail away when a storm's approaching, and somebody else—no one ever knew who—climbed up the Materada bell tower and begun ringing the bell wildly.

Milio told us all this in one breath, finally falling back in the chair, exhausted. When I saw the sun going down, I suggested he go home. "Don't be afraid. Let's go and vote, why don't we," I joked to give him courage. I went with him all the way down to the road and there in front of the elm tree suggested he take the Sterpín road, which cut through the fields and was the shortest.

I set off for home and got as far as the Barsetta field when I had the feeling I was being followed. I turned and saw three men in back of me. I recognized one of them as the youngest son of the Kersa family. They worked for us. I sped up a little, but they seemed in no hurry. They were walking slowly, breathing with difficulty as they climbed over the big rocks, like day laborers on their way to work. One of them laughed now and again. My heart was beating hard, yet I was calm— they didn't seem to be paying any attention to me. The sun had entered the sea and only a sliver of red remained above the Arrigoni factory in Umago. I began to hurry: I had to get the animals into the stable. They were following me step by step now. I turned at a ditch and went around a hedge; fifty paces back they turned at the same ditch and went around the same hedge. I stopped; they stopped. I went on; they went on.

I pushed open the cane gate to the vineyard below the house and—I don't know why, maybe to show we had no reason to be afraid and lock ourselves in—left it half-open. I went straight into the house. "Where's Uncle Matteo?"

"Out with the animals," said Berto. "He should be back any time now." My wife started asking whether Milio's story could be true. I left her and ran outside: they were under the oak tree by then, coming directly at me. So as not to stand there and wait for them, I pretended nothing was the matter and went into the stable. I stood still inside, waiting, remembering Milio's story. Without realizing it, I found myself holding a pitchfork. I heard the bells on the cows and steers outside and the clear voice of the Kersa boy, "*Ovaj*" (That's him), and my uncle crying out, "You bastards!"

I was about to walk out with the pitchfork, but the frightened animals coming into the stall blocked my way; over their backs I could see that Uncle Matteo had fallen to the ground and the two strangers were kicking him in the sides. When I finally made my way through the cattle, they had left him and were heading back. His neck was covered with blood. I called out to the Kersa boy, "You're the one responsible for this!" The one with the pistol was walking behind them, keeping it pointed. "Nobody asked your opinion," said the Kersa boy.

There was nothing for me to do but pick Uncle Matteo up and carry him to bed.

The beer and wine were slowly starting to affect Milio. He looked up at me with his tired eyes and said, "We've been through some stuff together, Cesco, old pal."

His gaze wandered through the tavern, where people were singing, laughing, clinking glasses. "What good is it?" he went on, shrugging. "What good is it that they've let up a little now or the two governments have shaken hands and put a consulate in Capodistria?"

He looked at Italo all sweaty in front of us, pouring beers from the tap, and at Lunardo, laughing and showing his gold tooth, while Old Man Nin yelled that he should have held onto the ace, and at old Sitar, talking to Marco at another table.

"You think all these guys will stay now that they're going to close the gate at Skofije for good? You think they'll stay here and wait for the next elections, for more blood, and trade the rights they'll have there for the ones they've lost here?"

Milio knew what he was talking about. It was a question of rights too. You could already hear about people who'd been in prison, and others whose son had died in the war, and still others whose father had been taken away one night, and now they were dusting off old documents, getting depositions, and going off to talk with a lawyer or with the Italian consulate in Capodistria.

Sure it was a matter of rights, I thought. That was what counted. And the cash they could expect to collect as soon as they got to Italy because of a blow from a club, or a case of

pneumonia, or a common cold. Some people were even looking through once useless pieces of paper, receipts, expired bills
of exchange, contracts, and pension booklets, which now, just
because there was something written in Italian at the top, had
assumed new importance.

I looked around at the people in the tavern as they laughed
and played.

The ones who, according to Milio, would leave were all
wearing something from Trieste—a tie, a jacket, a shirt—
things sent by relatives or, as everyone was saying, from the
Christian Democrats. And at home in their kitchen cup-
boards they were sure to have bags of pasta or ground sugar,
or lemons and oranges, which you couldn't find here, and rice
on Sundays. Maybe that was why their faces looked different
from the two or three who were part of the *skupčina* crowd,
which also gathered at Gelmo's. I saw Marco, who had always
been one of those most devoted to the Church and still
secretly came around collecting alms, and Lunardo, who had
spent time in prison along with Nando, the two of them
accused of having taken part in an expedition of fascists that
had gone to Maresego with clubs and broken open the barrels
in a cellar to let the wine out, and Sitar, who was accused of
having stolen gold jewelry from women in Greece; I saw that
their faces and others showed signs of outrages by the Titoists.
They could call themselves "refugees," as the people on the
coast certainly did, in Capodistria, for instance, where there
were so many students and where, after all, the Italian nationalist and war hero Nazario Sauro had been born.

But what about me? I had some cheap rags on, a kind of
sack that Uncle Matteo had bought at the agricultural cooperative, the *zadruga*, and a pair of thick, clumsy shoes that would
have been okay to wear ten years before. Besides, we spoke
Croatian at home, and during the last months of the war we
had helped the partisans. Then they'd made me secretary of the
local committee, though I didn't want to accept, and all I'd got
for my trouble was a slap in the face that some fascist from

Umago—that is, an Italian—had given me because I'd said two words in Croatian.

After that afternoon, the pain had grown so strong and heated in my chest that it made me want to stand up then and there in the middle of the tavern and cry out at the injustice of it, and they would have left their cards and drinks and felt sorry for me.

But all I could see and hear was a confused drone and a cloud of smoke and the sounds of chairs being moved and the movements of people immersed in their own lives. Then there was Milio, caught up in his own problems, turning them over again and again. "It doesn't make much sense for you to go, with all your land and stock," he said to me. "Even if you went to America, you could never get yourself fifty or sixty acres like what you've got here, the best in Materada."

He didn't know how pointed his words were. But I only patted him on the shoulder, smiled, and said, "You know I couldn't go."

■ □ ■ □ ■

IV

JUST THEN IN WALKED SANDRO BONAZZA. HE CAME STRAIGHT over to the bar, greeted us, and ordered himself a quarter-liter of wine from Italo. But Italo wasn't paying attention; he was playing with the dog again, calling it names, pulling its hair, laughing and making faces. Gelmo, who was carrying empty bottles back, shook his head and wondered aloud whether he or the dog had more sense.

"Hey, Italo! You'll have time for that later," Sandro shouted. "Pour me out a nice quarter-liter, eh? I got a frog here in my throat that just don't want to go down."

He put his hand on my shoulder, pulling me toward him, and winked. He asked whether we wanted to have a drink with him, but we still had a full bottle.

"Where are we off to in such a rush?" asked Milio.

"The ladies are outside waiting; they're itching to kick up their heels."

He was in high spirits.

He took out his wallet and started looking through it, taking pains to let the folded bills inside be seen. He wanted to pay with a thousand-dinar note, and Milio, who can never hold his tongue, said, "Take another look there, Sandro. Seems to me I saw a fifty."

"What's the difference?" he said. But Italo claimed not to have any change and wanted the fifty. Sandro opened his wallet again, shook his head as if to show how silly it all was, and paid. He had never owned land himself, having always taken day jobs, and now that he could count on regular work at the Promet, the trade center, in Umago, he wanted people to see he had his own thousand-dinar notes.

He began to sip his wine, savoring it. From the way he drank, you could tell it was precious, something that cost money.

"You feeling good today, Sandro, with all those big bank-notes in your wallet?" I asked.

Sandro pretended to be above it all. "It's just my weekly pay."

Milio turned to me, raising his chin, and said loudly, "See, Franz, buddy, there are no storms in his fields."

"I wish," Sandro rejoined. "I still got to get up every morning in the dark to make the five A.M. truck."

But he was happy, his eyes laughing, his hand on his wallet, the ladies waiting outside to go dancing. He felt strong, like a king. He turned to me and asked, "You coming to the dance?"

"I might look in for a while."

And out he went, his shoulders hunched forward.

"You notice the goings on?" Milio asked under his breath, indicating the table in the middle of the room. As soon as Sandro went out, Lunardo had stopped playing and asked Gelmo for the bill, while the others tried in vain to get him to play some more; he was ready to get up and go.

"You get it?" asked Milio, who was a real expert in such things.

"But I thought . . . ," I said unwillingly. "What about the other guy?"

"That guy's for every day, whenever she gets the urge. This other guy's top quality; he's for holidays. Come to think of it, didn't you used to go around with Femia?"

I was expecting the question. "A long time ago," I said. "Nothing serious. Kid's stuff really."

"She's quite a lady, I must say."

"There are better," I said. "Sure, when she was a girl. . . . She was like a flower."

Rozzan left the table where he'd been watching the game and came over to the bar.

"What's the use of starting if you're going to leave in the middle?" he said, facing Milio more than me. "Nobody even feels like playing, don't you think, hunchback?"

I wondered what Milio would say, but he didn't seem to care. He seemed to have one foot on the other side of the gate at Skofije, on *terra italiana*. All he did was shrug his shoulders and look down into his empty glass, his lips pressed tight.

Rozzan didn't get it and felt like joking around. Now he wanted to fraternize with everybody, I realized, especially people who'd steered clear of "the movement."

"What's the matter, hunchy?" he said. "Your bump hurting you?"

Milio was dead silent.

"What the devil's bothering you you don't answer?"

Still no response. I felt bad for him and said jokingly, "It's all the thinking."

"Actually, I did hear something. So you're leaving us, Milio? You're going?"

Milio's great moment had come. He pushed out his chest, his face looked beer drunk. He was smiling again maliciously. "Some can and some can't," he said provocatively. But Rozzan didn't get upset.

"What do you mean?"

"Just that. Some can and some can't."

"Can't what?"

"Go where they'd like to go."

"What kind of nonsense is that? Everybody can go wherever they like."

"Not everybody, Rozzan, not everybody," Milio went on, his voice low, as if he'd just got out of bed.

"So you're the only one who's got permission?" he said in Croatian. "You're a fine one to talk. Tell me who's keeping me, for instance, from going if I want?"

"You'll find out," said Milio in Italian.

"Why's that? I don't got just as much right to go as any-body else?"

"Not the way I see it."

"What's got into him!" said Rozzan. "Tell me, you lunatic: why the hell is it I can't go wherever I damn well please?"

"You'll find out."

I couldn't have acted like Milio. I don't have the courage for it. But something that evening was making me watch Rozzan as I never had before. I watched his blood-red face and his crew-cut hair, coarse as porcupine bristles; I looked for the hired laborer who'd broken with his boss once and for all, with paying him half the earnings. He'd wanted to be his own boss, and everyone else had followed his lead. So his house had become the home of the new regime, where any military man or civilian, anyone who wore the red star on his cap and brought the latest news, could go and get a glass of wine and a bowl of soup (the women would even put out a chicken and a bottle as if a prospective husband had come). And now, all done up in red, he was at the headquarters of the *skupčina*, where they gathered all the earnings like friars and divided them up later among themselves. They were the ones, I thought, who'd benefited from the last ten years: Rozzan and his compatriots, who could always collect, if with their fists, who could change holidays if they felt like it, and work, and marry off their children (but always at town hall), and run over to Buje for May Day, and rabble-rouse, and talk as loudly as they pleased. Cars no longer stopped at Nando's house, but they did at Rozzan's, where there had even been stores and *zadruga* offices before they'd built the Dom. They were the ones who'd taken the bull by the horns, and it seemed that Yugoslavia and communism itself had come to Istria just for them (like a cloud that brings no hail but only healthy rain to certain fields); to take somebody like Toni Lessio, who nobody had ever heard of before, pull him out of his little house, and make him chairman of the local committee, in short, god of the district; to put Nini Frajar into a car, Nini who had never even used a carriage so as not to tire out the one animal he kept alive by straw and curses; and to open the doors of the tavern to the people from Grotta and Vàrdizza who would eat a potato with two grains of salt and wait under the hen with their hands open to run to the shop while the egg was still warm and trade it for tobacco.

And not just them. It had also come for Miro Zupan, who'd squandered his entire property at cards (they returned it to him, the land that Bortolo had bought at auction), and for the Sossa brothers, who'd stripped every plant of its fruit while it was still in bloom and who were filthy inside and out and always barefoot (to them they gave a pair of shoes, a musket, and the title "Defenders of the People"); it had come, in short, for the down and out, who had the sole merit of owning nothing and of sleeping and eating God knows where, in the stables, in haystacks, or out in the open.

But the others, people who'd owned land and run the markets and bought and sold goods before the war, they had to be careful about having a party or singing or getting together. For them the ten years just passed had meant a continuous waiting, it had meant talking under their breath after putting their kids to bed, fearing their wives or their brothers or their own shadows, because times had changed, and it seemed everyone had gone crazy: people had their own ideas and interests to defend, and you heard about brothers who'd stabbed each other, a wife who'd denounced her husband.

But now unexpectedly things were finally beginning to change a little: there was that agreement in London, and the prewar atmosphere seemed to be returning. Marco and Sitar were talking freely at one table, the boys from Sferchi were singing in Italian, and Rozzan had returned, dejected, to the town's old tavern, where we all used to come to throw back a few and toss some confetti after our weddings and before the big receptions.

My brother came up and took Milio aside, and I found myself alone with Rozzan, who took me over to the corner amidst some empty beer casks. We hadn't talked up close like this for a long time, not since I'd resigned as secretary of the Popular Liberation Committee, and he and Giovanni Bože had asked me, "Are you sure, Franz?" and I'd answered, "I can't." A year later, they'd beat up my cousin Carlo at the fair in San Rocco of Verteneglio just after he'd returned from a concentration camp in Germany and stabbed Silvano from Petrovia thirteen times on his way back from the Buje fair, and I passed to the other camp once and for all.

"Well, Franz," said Rozzan, "it seems Milio's leaving too," and his voice seemed the old friendly one of ten years back. It was as if we'd stayed at the point where we'd left off and the time had come to sum things up.

"Seems like it," I, too, said in Croatian. And for a moment I felt quite close to him and full of courage, as if I had the power to turn those ten years around, start everything over, take charge of my fields, reap their harvest, buy my wife clothes, and send my son off to study.

"A lot of people are going to leave," said Rozzan. But he sounded different to me: an old man who felt abandoned, a little boy who couldn't keep up with the adults.

"At heart, they're right," he added, looking around. "Too many taxes, friend. People are tired. What've they seen all these years but work and more work? And what's the point? Where's the satisfaction?"

These were the kind of words that suited me, since in his eyes I was just a little, reactionary landowner. He wanted to test the waters to say other things, intimate things burning under his skin. By the way he was looking around and speaking softly (even if there was no need to), I understood he wouldn't, at least for the moment, be saying anything interesting. I wanted to see him now as the man he'd been ten years before, the Rozzan who, not even sitting at the head table, had only to stand and say two words to have everybody on his side. Now he was complaining too, and I decided to let him. He had clearly chosen a path for his speech, opened himself up, and I felt I had him in my hands. Like a reactionary landowner, I said, "Other people seem to have done all right."

"That's what you think," he said, trying to clear himself. "But if you want to know the whole truth. . . . At first, I don't deny it. But little by little we've gone back to when Ferluga was boss over my fields, when he'd come and weigh the grapes and calculate the profit to the last dinar. Worse than that. Before at least I could call that little bit my own, but now in the *skupčina*. . . . Look at these clothes I'm wearing! You could practically hang me on a tree like a scarecrow! I put thirty-five acres of land into that damned *skupčina,* and four steers; I gave them the wine cellar, the house, where they all come and go whenever they please. Is it right I should get the same out of it as Mitio Vesnaver or Vane or Gioachin, who didn't put a thing into it but their bare hands? Is it right that Ciano—because they made him director—should be in charge of my land and run around the offices in Buje and Capodistria with his nose in the air and a leather pouch under his arm? Or that I should be like some day laborer who gets his wine rationed? Is it right? Is it?"

I didn't answer. I couldn't forget that he was the one who had collected all the signatures of the workers who wanted to join the Materada "collective." He, along with Giovanni Bože and my cousin Franjo, had come to our house to persuade us to join the kolkhoz, promising, while Uncle Matteo was outside, to give my brother and me all the land and leave him only what he needed to survive. And now Rozzan was complaining.

I would like to have asked him just one thing: were they yours, the steers and land and house and wine cellar that you said you put into the *skupčina* and that you think give you more rights than Matio Vesnaver or Vane or Gioachin, those poor guys who had nothing to offer but their own bare hands?

He saw I was serious, so he went on softly: "My house has become communal property. Any outsider who comes to give us orders or chew us out, where does he eat and sleep? At Rozzan's. There's room for everybody. And who thinks of the cost? I work and slave the same as always, more than before, and for guys who can't make a decent graft, who don't want to work . . . And who's the new boss? Who's giving the orders, and who's taking them?"

So he wanted rights, too. It was only natural. But when I failed to respond, he took me brusquely by the arm, trying to turn it all into a joke. "Know what I say, Franz?" he asked. "One pope dies, another gets elected."

I looked at him as if to ask for an explanation, and he said sententiously, "What I mean is that when one boss dies, another one comes to take his place."

But by the way he had been talking, gesticulating, complaining, and calling for rights, I understood that not even he had realized how true his words were.

They called him to take Lunardo's place in the game and, still holding his arms out and complaining, but smiling all the while, he sat down contentedly at the card table in the old tavern, as he had before the war, next to three men who had remained the same bosses and reactionaries they had always been and were now on the point of leaving this "inferno" and going off to Trieste with their many rights, but who just then wanted only to enjoy their last few days here and finish out the hand, and who in their hearts had long since forgiven him.

Milio and Berto came over to my corner. They must have been talking about Rozzan the whole time, because their eyes questioned me maliciously.

"So what has our 'chief' got to say?" asked Milio. "Jumping for joy, is he? Everything okay with him?"

"Not quite everything," I answered. "As for the jumping part, wait till we get over to the Dom."

I paid for the other beers. Milio said he wanted to but then let me, though not before letting me see the inside of his wallet, just like Sandro Bonazza.

The table and bench outside were empty. Sabadin, I thought, must have lumbered off to the Dom to play the fool some more and entertain a new crowd.

■ □ ■ □ ■

V

WE COULD HEAR THE BAND PLAYING AND MEN SINGING AT THE
Dom from as far away as the school. The bar was in chaos:
everybody was running in, deserting poor Gelmo, especially the
young people, who wanted to play billiards, have a cold beer,
and buy their friends a drink, but still stay near the dance.

I saw my son there too, trying to act older than he was
with some friends, shouting and waving a fifty-dinar note to
get himself served quickly. When he saw me, he was ashamed
and instinctively lowered the fifty-dinar note he had finagled
from his mother. But it wasn't the money: he felt a little guilty
for coming to the dance after hearing what had happened at
home. Not wanting to spoil his time with his pals, I put on a
cheerful face, gave Milio a pat on the back, and asked, "What
are you treating me to, hunchy?"

But Milio had trained his little eyes on the group of "comrades" singing in Croatian, their arms interlocked for a *kolo*
dance. They had formed a circle under the big red star painted
in the middle of the ceiling and were rolling their heads from
side to side.

Two of the Kersa boys were there, Franjo's sons (one of
whom had become a teacher after two years of study), two boys
from Grotta, and a Navy officer who was stationed at Petrovia
and who had been coming to town to talk to Giovanni Bože's
daughter. They were singing songs no one had heard before,
stamping their feet and knocking over the empty beer bottles

they'd left under the tables. Watching them open-mouthed, red-faced, their hair down to their eyes, watching the officer setting the tempo, you realized they were the ones who had grown into maturity these last ten years and were intended for the reins of power. Milio was frowning like someone swallowing a very bitter wine. To keep his frown from attracting attention, I asked, "You think they'll be leaving too?"

He stood for a minute lost in thought, then said with certainty, "It won't be three months before you see them turn like the weather when the mistral's blowing."

Berto moved in close to listen. I took two steps back and stepped on somebody's foot. Turning, I saw my cousin Franjo. "Don't you see anybody when it's a holiday?" he said with a laugh.

"I didn't see you," I answered. "What's the holiday got to do with it?"

"I just meant when we change our clothes and the 'gentlemen' come into town with their wallets bursting."

He was already softened up from drinking, so I knew how to handle him. "Mine isn't bursting," I said, "but if you want a beer I can take care of that."

"Let's have one then," he said, pressing me to sit down with him. But Milio gave me a swift kick and I was barely able to hide the pain. "That's okay," I said. "I'm with some friends."

"Some friends," he replied immediately, though not loud enough for Milio to hear.

I watched him laugh, looked at his treacherous little face, and saw in him the adult version of the domineering boy who, lacking courage himself, goaded me and Berto, the strongest of the Croatians, into picking a fight with the boys from Cipiani and Petrovia, all Italians. When things turned bad, he found a way to come forward and say they were in the right. Now that he'd become party secretary and chief informer and in general the most trusted person they had in Materada, he could not have done better than to have pushed Gioachin into denouncing Nando at the tribunal in Buje, getting him two years hard labor and having everything he owned confiscated, while continuing to greet Nando's wife and kids as if nothing had happened. As I shoved my way through the crowd to the bar to order a beer for this man whom everybody had seen spend money left and right since the Liberation and never lift a finger for anyone, I thought that while we were of the same family and had the same surname, he was the only one of us all to benefit dishonestly from our Slavic origin.

Gino Juròn served me the beer. Only when I brought it over to Franjo and saw him stretch out his hand for it as if it were something he deserved, sitting there calmly like the parish priest, only then did I regret having done it. He seemed to be showing off the position he'd attained by taking a road I hadn't wanted to follow. I found it infuriating to see him enjoying it so and was on the point of telling him about Uncle Matteo and how Berto and I had been repaid for agreeing to follow him and stay on his side while Franjo had told us a thousand times just what we should do, and had even come with Rozzan and Giovanni Bože all the way to Monte to offer us land as long as we entered the *skupčina* along with them.

I put the beer down in front of him, banging it hard. "Your beer, sir," I said.

"Sir?" came his ready response. "There are no more 'sirs' here. We sent them all packing to Trieste. If anyone's a 'sir,' it's you for paying."

He laughed so hard at his own cleverness that Nini Gazde (he, too, had a son studying in Fiume or Zagreb) came up to him and wrapped his arm around his neck, laughing along with him without knowing why.

"To my cousin Franz," Franjo said, filling Gazde's glass.

To show his gratitude, Gazde felt obliged to ask about my uncle's health.

"He pulled through," I answered, feeling the color in my face.

Franjo covered my embarrassment by saying, "And he's so happy he's been treating everybody."

"Sure," I said. "Shouldn't I be?"

He stared at me, disappointed. "Isn't he leaving everything to you?"

I stared back to see whether something had reached his ear.

"The house, the livestock, the land . . . ," he said, counting on his fingers.

"Why to me alone?" I asked, not letting him finish. "He's got a son too."

"Yeah, but he took off. Means he's not interested in his father or his father's belongings. Anyway, I can't believe the old man would play a dirty trick like that on you. Not after you've buttered him up all these years."

"I can't either," I said, going over to Milio.

Berto was ready to boil over. I could see by the way he was glued to Milio that things had turned sour and he was about to blurt everything out. So I slipped between them and signaled to Milio to look over at (as he called them) "our comrades." From the corner near the door, where you passed on your way to the toilets and then on to the other rooms and offices of the *zadruga*, you could see everybody in the bar, huddled together: the promising young sons, singing and dancing the *kolo* in the center, and their respected fathers, seated at the tables—Toni Jurisević, Taviano Sossa, Kudela, the Martinčić brothers, Old Man Kersa, and others, all men who, as far back as the Austrian monarchy, had had their share of troubles, pitted against Old Man Nin and his intrepid friends from the Lega Nazionale. Now, after years and years of waiting and silence, they had finally made it in a way. The atmosphere, with the red star on the ceiling and the songs in Croatian and Gino Juròn yelling "*molim, molim*" from behind the bar (though without Gelmo's ulterior motive), could be said to be complete. Milio pointed his chin and said, "Look at our friends. Look at our comrades." Then making another stab at wit, he added, "And they're all in your house."

"Mine? Only mine?" I asked, joining in the spirit of his joke. "Isn't it the people's? Isn't it everyone's?"

"No, yours," he insisted. "You helped build it."

"Just listen to him," I said, turning to Berto. "Now that he's leaving, he thinks he can play everybody for a fool. Didn't you bring in twenty wagonloads of stones of your own?"

"Sure," he said. "I belong to the people, too, don't I?"

We were quiet for a moment. Then I slipped my arms into theirs and pulled them outside, saying, "Then we've all got the right to dance!"

The ballroom of the Dom was so big that despite the young people dancing in the middle—they'd come from the small towns throughout the district—and the two lines of benches on either side filled with all their mothers, the room still seemed half-empty. The musicians had their instruments on their knees and were passing a drink around, Fioravante pouring it from a flask and shaking his big shiny head all the while. The first thing we saw when they started playing again was Ciano Benolić making a scene with poor Sabadin. Ciano was dancing with him, holding him tight and petting him as if he were a girl, while Sabadin was as serious as could be, trying not to look drunk. Four slick youths were circling them, clapping their hands. Everybody was laughing, bumping into them on purpose, while Ciano, chairman of the collective farm, winked at them to show how everyone was in on the joke and to invite people to dance along. Only a few couples in love pulled away, wanting to act respectable. Suddenly Giovanni Bože appeared out of the clutter and took me by the arm, his eyes laughing.

"What you see in Materada," he said, "you won't see anywhere else in the world."

"True," I answered, "but there's things to be ashamed of too."

"There's no harm meant; they're just joking."

"Sure, to keep things merry. But the other guy deserves to have his head smacked."

"Why?" said Milio abruptly. "You think he's any better than Sabadin?"

A line of young people had formed. They joined hands and moved shouting and stamping their feet toward the two men bouncing up and down. As they collided, Ciano let go and poor Sabadin careened four steps into the wall, where he fell among the feet of the old ladies who had been watching their daughters dance and who now jumped up screaming. There was nothing but laughter and pats on the back for Ciano, who stood there like a champion. Even the musicians had risen to their feet, playing as well as they could. Sabadin was still on the ground, his big lamb eyes searching for someone to help him up, but everybody just kept pointing at him and laughing, and the women on the bench had huddled together, forming a single black blot.

The poor man finally picked himself up and, amidst new cries of laughter, shuffled over to his friend, calling out his name, inviting him to continue, and shaking his head like an obstinate mule. But Benci, the dance organizer, intervened, taking Sabadin by the arm and shoving him toward the exit. When Sabadin resisted, Benci lifted him off the ground and carried him out in his arms. Sabadin, up in the air, bared his chest and worked his fists, threatening a boy who'd done nothing wrong, calling him to step outside; he'd be waiting for him in the street.

People were beside themselves with laughter. Seeing Berto and Milio and Giovanni Bože laugh so hard, I couldn't help laughing myself, though with my mouth clenched. (Things like this happened every time there was a dance, and I often found them funny. It was different this time, though: the more I kept the secret to myself, the more I looked on like a stranger, unable to take part.)

"There's other things to laugh at, boys," I said. "Let's go." And as I passed Giovanni, I said, using his Croatian name, "I've got something to tell you, Ivo. I'll be back."

Two trumpet blasts announced that the band was playing once more, and we moved further into the dance room.

Sandro Bonazza ran by at that point, waving us ahead. He was shuffling around in front of his daughter, and from the way he talked, moved, and looked about, you'd have thought he was the one running the dance. His wife, Femia, was dancing with Lunardo, who stared like an ostrich into her eyes and smiled, showing his gold tooth. He nodded at us, still smiling, to say he'd be right with us. Sandro and his daughter were waiting for the waltz to end, and Milio's glances had become more malicious than ever. There was nothing for me to say, so I simply watched the youngsters dance and caught softly spoken words, like warm puffs of a southeast breeze, and short bits of laughter over the din of the clarinets and trumpet. My son was standing under the bandstand gazing up, entranced, not yet daring to dance. I realized he was at that first stage of dance-going, when you think all the fun and celebrating is up there on the bandstand with the musicians and their instruments; not until later do you learn you've got to enter into the life of the room, mingle with the people, ogle the women, choosing one and putting yourself forward; and you're sorry a little.

When the musicians finished playing, most of the dancers returned to their places along the benches. Those who stayed in the middle, talking and holding hands, were engaged couples or other young men with girls in their meshes. Red in the face, Femia was fanning herself with her hands: Lunardo was standing like a tough guy in the middle of the floor, telling Sandro how great she still was, and light as a feather, so much so that he'd thought he was dancing with a girl.

"A girl past forty," she said, laughing.

I could hear in her voice, as I looked at the lines in her forehead and around her eyes, how little she believed what others said: she was the only one who knew her true measure. And looking more closely, I wondered what was left of the young girl I'd stretched out in the hay those moonlit nights. Did she remember the letters I'd sent her from the service, and the last one when I told her I was breaking it off because of the bad things people were saying about her?

"You're lucky they don't have postcards tonight," said Milio. "If they had, you'd have been chosen queen."

"Why?" she said laughing. "Wouldn't you have bought me a postcard?"

"Sure," he replied, "every postcard for sale at Vestro's."

People were saying that she'd been making out with Vestro, a man who worked at the cooperative. But no one got Milio's joke, and I thought that Femia's good fortune was in fact a disgrace. A woman lets herself go, she chooses to follow that life, and everybody thinks they have the right to talk about her like a thing, and no slaps will help. If she knows this—that you lose so much for so little and become something common, in words if not in deeds—why does she let herself be thrown away? I can understand when it's out of need and a way of earning a living. But what did Femia need? How many opportunities had she had to get married, earn money, have her children, and run a household? But instead she'd wanted to do just as she saw fit. What my poor mother had written me when I was in the service was confirmed by everyone in person: when I came back, she didn't want to talk to me, not even to explain herself. We would see each other—"hello," "good-bye," "how are you" at most—and that was it. But by then she was doing it publicly, out of spite maybe. When the war was over and Sandro Bonazza came back from Corsica, they went out a couple of times. They were both unmarried, both out of work and penniless. They were married during the grape harvest, and every night for a week a mob from the surrounding towns came to bang empty gas cans or chamber pots under their windows, and they made such a racket that the whole district heard it.

The musicians started playing again. The shameless Lunardo wanted to dance with her some more, but Sandro used his authority to tell him it was my turn to take Femia for a round.

I objected, and even their daughter was ashamed and started complaining she was tired and would he ask Mama to come home.

Femia leaned over her and all but gave her a slap. She said she'd settle with her when they got home and just let her ask to be taken to another dance.

So I had to accept and play the fool, as tired and nauseated as I was from the atmosphere and the day and everything.

Sandro was clapping his hands, marking time to the waltz, content to be in command; Milio and Berto were laughing, Lunardo was forcing himself to laugh, my son had turned his back and was pretending not to know me, and Fioravante was winking at me from above his baritone sax. But what offended me most was that Femia kept looking for Lunardo over my shoulder and was dancing with me just to strike a pose. I thought then that everybody ought rightly to have done to me what they'd wrongly been doing to Sabadin shortly before.

We finished the waltz. Femia was all sweaty. I didn't wait for a second; I had to see Giovanni Bože about something. Everybody teased me, saying that wasn't the way things were done and what sort of a man was I to be scared by a woman.

"I've got to go," I said. Berto understood.

I went back to the front building of the Dom and saw Sabadin sitting at the entrance, in the midst of people passing between the bar and the toilets and going upstairs to the *zadruga* offices. His bare foot rested on a shoe. As I came closer, I noticed that it was inflamed and that he was crying silently, his great slobbering mouth wide open. I asked him what had happened. Haltingly, his words broken by sobs, he said he had sprained it running after the boys from Montelici. The sprain didn't mean a thing, he explained, but those boys shouldn't treat their elders like that. Ciano had told him they'd gone to mount his wife in Materada, and now he didn't know what to do. He wanted to go home, but he'd tried to walk and couldn't; he was waiting for Ciano to come for him with a cart.

It must have happened right after they'd kicked him out of the dance, because he seemed to have been waiting there forever.

"I'll be back in a minute," I said and ran up the stairs, reflecting that it gave me another reason to knock at Giovanni Bože's door.

His quarters were just beyond the *zadruga* offices. I found everyone in the kitchen, even the officer from Petrovia who had removed his holster and was talking to Giovanni's daughter while Giovanni's mother-in-law circled him, constantly refilling his glass with grappa.

"Giovanni," I said. "Poor old Sabadin is downstairs. He can't walk."

"Tell him to drink less."

"It's not that. He fell, or somebody pushed him."

"Ciano's gone for the carriage to take him home."

"Maybe we ought to call the Red Cross. His foot's swollen bad."

"Fine. They find him drunk, and what do we look like? Ciano will take him home, he'll sleep it off, and tomorrow morning he'll jump out of bed like a young rooster."

"I have something else to talk to you about, Giovanni."

"By all means," he said, leading me into the dining room.

We had a drink, talked about this and that, and then I told him the story.

"What does he intend to leave to you?" he asked.

"The Kerso property."

He, too, couldn't help laughing. "The old smart-ass," he said. "And what do you plan to do?"

"I'm asking you. Aren't you the new priest?"

He smiled and said, "You always find a way to show your resentment, Franz."

"But you and I are friends. You've always said so."

"And I say so now. But I can't do anything for you, Francesco. This is a serious business. Your uncle has all the land registered in his name.

"Anyway, what difference does it make?" he asked, squinting at me as he smoked. "You work the land, so it belongs to you. Other people think of it that way, even if they don't deserve to."

"Thanks a lot," I said, "but I want the land to be mine. I want to do with it what I please."

"You can have what it yields."

"That's not enough. Anyway, I can't accept something I haven't agreed to. I can see taking things away from people with too much, but others ought to be able to keep what's theirs."

"People will say you're right, you'll see."

"What I want is a signed piece of paper saying I'm right, not people saying I'm right."

"It'll be hard," he said, rising. "Tomorrow you can see the judge."

I thought for a moment and said, "I will."

I said good-bye to the people in the kitchen and went down the stairs. The chair in the entrance was empty. I lit up a cigarette by the window. A dark shadow darting toward the acacia thicket beyond the school caught my attention. A man followed a few paces behind, moving confidently. I recognized him. I could even make out his gold tooth flashing in the moonlight. "Damn it," I blurted under my breath. I decided to go home without calling my brother, just to pass the two of them talking quietly, acting as if there were nothing unusual going on.

BUJE WAS THE CAPITAL OF THE WORLD TO US. ALL THE DISTRICT offices and courts were there. Buje was where cases were heard and prices determined. Buje was where the new holidays were celebrated with great pomp and circumstance.

I arrived drenched in sweat just after dawn, my legs aching because the town is perched on a hill. Rightly did our forefathers sing, "Buje stands as sentinel on its gentle mountaintop!"

Once past the fountain, I took the old road where the base of San Sebastian stands. Some men were already in the fields; others were riding down into the valley on the small, black donkeys typical of the region.

Even though the clerks wouldn't arrive until eight o'clock, the hall of justice vestibule was packed as usual. Almost everyone there had land or had lost land. Some were negotiating with the local cooperative to get it back; others were bringing suits against family members or acquaintances who had unexpectedly turned to the other side. When discussing the reactionary movement at conference meetings, they called them "the people who know only how to run to court." "Our workers," they would say, "have no need of courts because justice comes from them—they themselves are justice."

An old woman from Crassiza was speaking for everyone. "My poor husband—they killed him. My son never came home from the war. What more do they want from me? Why can't they give me what's mine?"

"Was it land that went up for auction?"

"It was the devil—may he swallow them all."

In the hall where so many people had been tried merely for opening their mouths (Nando for having said that when Italy took over he would chop off the heads of the local "representatives"), today you could speak as openly as you pleased—at least until the clerks arrived. Then there was no time to lose. Everyone pushed toward the door of the judge, the *sudac,* arguing over who went first. The judge, a learned, competent man, had his own troubles: listening to cases every day, trying various remedies that afterward came to nothing because the local committees had absolute authority and in effect decided the law. But he found the right words for each person lodging a complaint, which itself was a sign of his learning. With me he spoke even more freely since I had come to complain about a private individual.

"But Mr. Koslović," he said, "the court can do nothing in such matters. Your uncle has broken no law, in terms of either the land he received as inheritance or the land he acquired through normal commercial transactions. It is rather a case for his conscience."

"But he has no conscience, Your Honor."

"I can see that. But what can we do about it? Ask him to come and see me, and I'll try to make him see reason."

"I'm afraid you won't succeed for all your skill. And, Your Honor, I believe I have a right to what's mine. . . ."

I couldn't go on: a sob had come into my throat because he was so good to me and was listening to me and treating me like an equal. He patted me on the shoulder and, dismissing me, said, "Go into the front office and have the secretary write an invitation to your uncle. You can take it to him yourself or send it if you like."

"But he'll refuse to come."

He thought for a moment, then opened the door decisively and said, "Well, then we'll have him come by force."

I took the invitation from the outer office and left content. The judge was on my side. He had said my uncle was in the wrong and spoken to me as an equal. I went down to the Lama for a beer.

Many people were waiting there for the buses to Umago and Cittanova. I took the eleven-fifteen bus and was home by noon.

Uncle Matteo had just come in from the pasture and was sitting at the door. He had seen me leave early, in my Sunday best, and had caught whiff of something. I took the invitation from my pocket, waved it in front of his nose, and said, "Here, Uncle Matteo. You've been summoned to the Justice Office in Buje."

"Who's summoned me? I have nothing to talk to a judge about. My papers are in order."

"Well, read it yourself. That's your name, isn't it. It says you're to report a week from today at nine A.M."

"Who's summoned me?"

"What do you mean? You've been summoned."

He stared at me severely, his eyes narrowing. "Your bosses have told you to grumble to the judge, haven't they?"

"Why not, since we can't deal reasonably with you. As for the leaders, I believe they're on our side."

"Adopting their methods, are you?"

"And whose methods did you adopt?"

I saw Berto coming in from the fields with my son. "Hey, Berto, come over here!" I called out loudly. "Listen, I've been to see the judge. Half of this land is ours, and nobody's going to take it away. Here I've brought an invitation for our uncle to report in a week's time."

"Good. We'll communicate better there."

"Communicate on your own. You're on the other side now. I'll stay here and wait for orders."

"That means they'll take you by force."

And they did.

Two weeks later two men from the People's Militia knocked at the door, asking for Matteo Koslović.

"I am Matteo Koslović," he said.

"We have orders to take you with us," they said.

"Why should I? I haven't killed anyone."

"Orders are orders."

And out they took him. We followed, not knowing whether to laugh or cry, but we walked with our heads down.

At Giurizzani we waited for the bus in front of the tavern. Old Man Nin was reading the paper under his elm. When he saw us he blew his nose and shook his head as if a gadfly were buzzing around him. He had seen Nando and Sitar dragged off just that way, except their hands had been tied.

Bortolo called me aside. "What do they want?" he asked. "Why are they taking you?"

On that day the People's Militia made me brave rather than afraid or embarrassed. "It's not us," I responded. "It's my uncle."

"Has something happened?"

"No, nothing," I said, "but the time for justice has come."

"I won't ask any more," he said, withdrawing into his shoulders and starting on his way.

Gelmo came out. I had seen him spying on us for some time behind his shutters. He understood immediately what was up. Raising his cap to us and, all friendly smiles and disinterest, he went straight to Uncle Matteo and said, "Can I offer you a chair, Tio?"

"I don't need any chair of yours," Uncle Matteo answered, turning his head.

"No offense meant. Just thought I'd ask," said Gelmo, and headed slowly back inside, savoring his victory at every step.

The judge sat us down and began by explaining to my uncle that he had not brought him there on a legal matter; he wanted to have an honest conversation with him and resolve a case of conscience. But Uncle Matteo immediately began pleading his case, waving his hands and asking if the judge was not charging him with wrongdoing, why had he brought him there by force, like a bandit, a *kolarić*?

"Let's move on, Mr. Koslović," said the judge, laughing. "No one has harmed a hair on your head. We simply knew you wouldn't have come otherwise, especially since you believe yourself blameless before the law. This case, I repeat, has more to do with your conscience."

From as far back as I could remember, Uncle Matteo had followed every legal proceeding he could. He knew the law as well as the judge. Nor was he the sort to let himself be taken in hand; he had a reply to everything. "If I am at ease before the law," he said to the judge, "then I am at ease with my conscience."

The judge swallowed. "I don't dispute that, but we don't feel that to be the case here, Mr. Koslović. You see, one must not be concerned solely with one's own conscience (since each of us has his own way of living and thinking and what is bad for me may be good for you and vice versa) but also with the conscience of us all. Of me (not as a judge), of your nephews (not as litigants in a suit), of the secretary here, of the people waiting outside. If you view things in this manner, you'll see that your nephews are entitled to half the land that is currently, by misfortune or neglect or pure chance, all under your name."

"Permit me please, Your Honor. You claim that the land belongs to this person and that. But can you prove it? Are you familiar with the affairs of our family? On what ground did you accept the word of a man who came here to complain, taking advantage of my ill health and of the fact that I'm too old to run around getting people to put things over on people?"

"You've put things over on people for too long as it is," said Berto.

Red in the face, the old man turned on him. "I've told you before, Berto—watch how you talk to me. It would take very little for me to sue you for the way you've slandered me and raised your fist against me."

Things were getting out of hand. "None of your arguments, please," the judge intervened. "Mr. Koslović, do you or do you not understand that depriving your nephews of their property is unjust?"

He had spoken rather abruptly, so the old man changed his tone and, joining his hands together, said plaintively, "But Comrade Begović, who wants to deprive them of their property? Don't you see? My two nephews, whom you are protecting because you believe they're in the right, they have their own land. And the truth is their land is actually much better than mine. Ask anybody who knows."

The judge's mouth dropped open.

"This is nothing new, Your Honor," I said. "He's talking about land that's under the Agrarian Reform."

"But that's land they can make no use of!" said the judge angrily.

"Well, then," my uncle answered, "instead of making an old man like me come all the way here to Buje, you should call together the Materada *skupčina* leaders and have them reinstate the land because it's land we bought fair and square. We didn't steal it from anyone!"

The judge shook his head. "This is no way to have a conversation, Mr. Koslović. You see, if you and I own a vineyard jointly (let's say you own the land and I do the work) and we work together to take in half the harvest, but then hail unexpectedly spoils half the grapes, how should we divide things? Is it right for you to take the half that was saved and leave the dry stems unfit for vinegar to me?"

"No, of course not."

"Well, isn't this the same thing?"

"No, not in the least. First, because no such storm has come and the land is the same as it always was, even if the workers in the collective don't know how it ought to be farmed. And second, if you consider the land reform and the whole movement of the past ten years as a mere storm or misfortune we must simply resign ourselves to, well, I won't argue."

At that point the judge lost his patience and his face reddened. "You're a malicious man, Mr. Koslović. My example was only that; I merely wanted to point out your error."

The judge spread his arms exactly as he had during Nando's trial, when Gioachin had first declared that yes, the accused had in fact said he would cut off the heads of the representatives; and then, hearing the protests of Nando's wife and children, that no, it wasn't true: he had been asked to say so, but actually Nando had not said those things; and then, at a glance from Franjo, who was also giving evidence for the prosecution, yes, he repeated, it was true, but he may have been joking or was drunk.

The public prosecutor had finally cut him off (if only to quiet the crowd, which was murmuring and laughing: one of the youngsters had cried out, "Don't believe him! He's the one who's drunk!") and asked, "So you think we ought to condemn him?"

At another glance from Franjo, the poor man dropped his head and muttered, "If he did say it, . . . you decide," and then, "Yes, condemn him."

It was then that the judge spread his arms, as if to say, "There's nothing I can do. You've brought this evil on yourselves. Make your own peace."

I had understood then, as I understood now, how just those unspoken words were. Throughout our troubles, throughout the battles and miseries of that sad period, I could see the hand of our own people at work. The examples were legion. There was always someone among us to point out the house earmarked for the beatings or destruction, someone among us to recall Nando's words or report that a man from Radini had harvested his barley for fodder and thus harmed the national economy, or denounce someone as a fascist who had broken open wine barrels in the cellars. They, the regime that is, had imposed a new set of laws, a new system, and to make it work they had lent (to the Franjos and Bencis and Toni Lessios, who knew how to turn the system to their advantage) the strong arms of men who had undergone the fascists' torture by castor oil and who had seen the wine flow from broken barrels.

There was nothing more to say to the judge. He stood up and accompanied us to the door. In a last-ditch attempt, he said to Uncle Matteo, making a special effort to speak our dialect, "Think it over, Tio. You have two fine nephews here. They could help you in your old age. Do what's right: come and see me and we'll make a legal transcript of the land you intend to leave."

"If you mean the Kerso property, I'm ready right now."

"That's no way to talk, Tio," he said, opening the door.

I stopped him and said, "I'd just like to know one thing, Your Honor. Is there a law in your region that will give me the rights to my land?"

"In this case there is not."

"Then in Buje or, say, Pola, or Zagreb?"

"Not even in Belgrade."

"Thank you very much, Your Honor."

Down in the street, the two of us left Uncle Matteo to the devil and headed for the Lama. We went into the bar that had once belonged to Nino Siroti but was now a "People's House." We sat in a corner, sad and discouraged. My brother kept biting his lower lip. We couldn't talk without breaking into tears or swearing. I kept replaying the conversation in my mind.

Naturally, I thought, to have free rein for whatever they felt like doing, all our friends from home had to do was attend the festivals in Buje, the great capital. They had only to show our superiors how many people they'd brought carrying flags and posters written in Croatian. It was just like '48, when the Allied delegation had passed through to draw the Istrian borders and there was not a single Italian flag to be seen, not even with a red star. No, there were signs saying "We want Yugoslavia" and "We are all Croats" all over the place. The pro-Yugoslavia shouting overwhelmed the delegation members: Englishmen, Americans, Russians, and Frenchmen. How could they doubt what the true desire of the Istrians was? Nando had pretended to be sick, but they'd hauled him out of bed, and he walked next to me in a cold sweat, hiding as best he could (eyes, nose, mouth) behind the cane that the daughter of one of his farm workers had shoved into his hand. It had a red flag fluttering from it.

Through the bar window I could see the remains of the recent May Day celebration: flags, posters, leaflets all over the ground, a grandstand, and a huge portrait of Tito on the facade of the Croat school. But where were the May Day celebrations when people from the whole district converged on Buje and all our Rozzans, bursting with happiness and stuffed with beer and sausages, trudged along with our supreme leaders as if their pants were full of shit?

They would set out in squads from the neighboring towns before sunup. Some traveled by wagon, others by truck, still others by bicycle or on foot. Like it or not, May Day was our Christmas and Easter, our Ascension Day and Corpus Christi. In '49 I came with Milio. Every village was supposed to form a group and join other groups in the towns. The villages around Materada gathered at Giurizzani, which could be called their natural center. People lined up the wagons with their flags flying: little paper ones on the sides, a large one out of cloth on the pole otherwise used to balance the load. The Cranzis had painted red stars on the steers' foreheads and the red, white, and blue stripes of the Yugoslav flag on their horns. In short, it looked like the end of the world, and eyeing the poor animals all decked out like that—as if they were drunk on wine and grappa too, yet walking as seriously and superbly and slowly as ever—I thought of the old proverb: joke with the jokers and leave the saints alone.

Everyone was in work clothes. The Cranzis wore their hats inside out, which men did during the war to pass themselves off as crazy and avoid being recruited; they even stripped completely and ran through the haystacks with just their hats on and big turkey feathers in them and sprigs of rosemary and sage. The Cranzis had unearthed an antique Victrola from an attic, the kind with a funnel-shaped speaker, and they turned it loud whenever they stopped, playing the Workers' Anthem and other marches they had loaned out from the People's House in Buje. Their wagon, first in line, sported a large sign that said "Materada": they were taking our official delegation. Out in front, of course, there was a band marching like at a funeral.

We joined the groups from Buroli and Carsette at Tramòn, everyone yelling and laughing, eager to get there, to be first.

At Buje it was quite a spectacle to see the long white street, which cuts through woods and fields to descend like a snake to the sea, strewn with colorful people and wagons, a long procession none of us had ever dreamed of. Members of the People's Militia showed us where to go. The bands left us and headed for the Lama, where they gathered under the big-wigs' grandstand. But the people in wagons had to pass through the marketplace and go all the way down to the station. We waited two long hours in the sun amidst the din and the songs as new wagons with signs like ours indicating the towns they were from poured in. The place was slowly turned into an open-air livestock market, the peasants tossing their steers handfuls of hay now and then and the animals tugging so hard at their harnesses that out came the whips and the inevitable curses.

The peasants, who enjoyed the celebration as much as Milio and I did and who were used to making the rounds at marketplaces, went from wagon to wagon, fingering the steers, looking them over at length, discussing whether they were purebred or not. A man from Levade came up to us and, after admiring the *skupčina* oxen, which weighed more than fifteen hundred pounds, said to Milio, "Fine specimens! Where they from?"

"Can't you read, friend?" Milio answered, pointing. "It's on the sign."

By then the bands were on their way to meet us, the brass instruments glittering from far off and people playing however they felt. Fioravante said later that you couldn't call it playing really and that to make music you needed much more, not just blowing any old way or as loud possible: they might just as well have beat on hoes and tin cans, like on the wedding night of a woman who's had her share of fun.

The procession left from the Lama and was supposed to make the rounds of Buje. First came the flags, then the officials, then the music and the wagons with signs and animals. A great shouting contest started up: long live, down with, death to. People clapped and screamed, partly out of enthusiasm, partly because they'd had some drinks at home, the bars and taverns being closed. It was all a little upsetting, a little frightening. In fact, I was really quite frightened.

I walked as if drunk—not even Milio felt like joking anymore—looking at the people, all from my own hometown, who used to let themselves go a little during carnival, but who now shouted with parched throats and hateful eyes as if the shouts had been hidden away in their chests for years and years waiting for the right moment to burst out. And I asked myself what had happened. Had the world gone topsy-turvy? Would this be the end of it?

But then I saw people whose faces had once been dark from hunger and who had looked on tearless as sons and sisters died, people who had been forced to eat field garlic and now had received something—some more, some less. And I felt that I, too, could have screamed like that.

The celebration ended at the moment the district president opened his arms, smiling blissfully like a woman in love, and said, "My dear friends!"

Once they'd had enough, "our people" set out for home, still singing and shouting as if they'd accomplished a feat or simply performed a duty and in exchange received the warm handshakes of some very important people.

And now, sitting in the bar and watching my brother Berto's face getting darker and harder, I wondered what was left of those great May Day festivities. Now everybody celebrated May Day in his own region, quietly, like a normal holiday, organizing competitions and sack races, the way the priest used to do for confirmations or the August fairs. Now, like when you plow, the earth had been dug up and what was underneath before had suddenly been brought to the surface and was lying there enjoying the sunlight, ready to accept the new seed and make it grow. The major part was over: in that very piazza they had put up a memorial plaque that depicted a man plowing and read, "All Land to the Peasants! An End to Agricultural Servitude. Buje, November 3, 1947." That was why you could sing a gondolier's song now and go off to Italy if you liked—it no longer hurt anybody. And here they were going on to me about laws and conscience.

We sat for a while in silence. Then I caught my brother's eye. He clenched his fists and said, his voice low, "You know, Francesco? Even if it means kicking the old bastard out, even it means burning down the house and going to prison, the land must be ours."

"Take it easy, Berto," I said. "If we're tough enough with him, he'll have to give up something. You'll see."

We went outside and got on the bus with people crowding one another and trampling the leaflets, shoving and yelling now merely to go back to their own affairs, pulling out their wallets and paying for their tickets.

VII

WE CONTINUED TO WORK AS ALWAYS, AND THE TIME SOON came to harvest the wheat. I stopped my uncle on the threshing floor, where I was cutting thorn bushes and other weeds so I could store the sheaves there. I hemmed and hawed a little because we hadn't spoken since that day in Buje.

"It's time to cut the wheat, Uncle Tio," I said. "How should we go about it?"

"Don't trouble yourself about me. You harvest what's yours."

"Excuse me, but whose land was it we plowed and seeded and fertilized?"

"Your efforts will be rewarded," he answered.

"That's no way to talk."

We were alone, he and I, under the oak, as so often before.

"Listen, Uncle Tio. We're all alone. Just you and me. I've given you no cause to speak ill of me. I've always listened to you. Now I want to talk about the wheat. Let's leave the land and the other problems out of it for the time being. Practically everyone else has finished harvesting, and if we wait any longer we'll be fattening up all the birds in the neighborhood. How are we going to split things?"

He sat down on a log left for firewood and answered haltingly, "Half and half. With the wheat we can go half and half."

"Half is dead already. How can we talk about half? One-third for you. It's plenty."

"None then. Who are you to make demands? What did you put into it?"

"My sweat. I seeded it, I hoed it, I put out the salt, I plowed the earth. And you? What did you put in?"

"The salt, the fertilizer, the seeds. And the most important thing."

"What's that?"

"The land."

At that point I blew up. "Son of a bitch, so that's it! Well, if you want to know what I think, you didn't put anything at all into it because the fertilizer and everything else you bought with our labor!"

He hadn't expected me to raise my voice and started in again playing the old man and complaining of his troubles. "You're just like your brother. Attacking me like this. What kind of gratitude is that after all I've done for you. I brought you up big and strong. And you have me put under guard like a thief. Don't trouble yourself about the wheat or about anything else. There are plenty of people who'll work the land without making unreasonable claims on other people's property."

And off he went, while I stared after him, mouth open and scythe in hand.

I got up late the next day: the sun was already up over the Buje hill. The air was fresh and sparrows chirped in the acacia beneath my window.

I could make out the fields of wheat and grapevines, the olive groves and spots of forest that stretched all the way to the seashore, where factory chimneys were smoking. Glancing toward Grotta, I was transfixed. At first it didn't register: I thought it was someone running after an animal in the wheat; then I thought it was a thief. At last I saw there were two of them and they were reaping, resting every so often, then taking up their work once more.

I ran into the old man's room but he wasn't there. I woke Berto and told him to hurry: they were harvesting the grain in the Rebro field. "Bring the scythes!" I said.

We were in the field in a flash, our wives and children with us.

Uncle Matteo was sitting under the cherry tree. He stood the moment he caught sight of me. The two day workers (one was Bepi from Portole, who had turned up at our place in years past in search of greener pastures, while the other, also from the hinterland, worked for the Fiaschis in Pizzudo) stopped and stared at us too.

"Another of your tricks, Uncle Matteo," I said.

By then Berto was in the wheat with his scythe.

"Stop working there," he shouted, "or you'll have me to deal with!"

It was like a lightning rod. I recalled how years before Nando and other landowners had woken up to find strangers harvesting the fields they had planted. But now the situation was completely different: it was even reversed.

"Wait!" I called to Berto. "What do they have to do with it?"

It occurred to me Nando had lacked the courage to cry out like that because the workers had attacked him and whipped his horse. And before I could turn, Berto, brandishing the scythe in his closed fist, had covered the distance to Uncle Matteo.

"What do you think you're doing, you bastard!" the old man yelled.

"Finishing you off once and for all!"

I cried out, my wife cried out, my sister-in-law cried out, and the children, and the two day workers. Two more steps and he would be on top of him.

"Put down that scythe, Berto!" I screamed.

Berto did as I said, but grabbed the old man by the collar and flung him to the red earth. Standing above him, his eyes crazed, he cried with all the voice he had, "See what I could do to you?! I could cut you into pieces so tiny your ear would be the biggest piece left!"

I managed to grab him by the arm, but he tried to pull away, bellowing even louder than before.

"Enough, Berto! We're not alone here. Stop this immediately or I'll have to teach you a lesson!"

But he pulled so hard it hurt. "What are you going to do?" he screamed. "You're afraid of your own shadow, you idiot! Letting him eat you out of house and home!"

I struck him so hard that he, too, fell to the ground. "Now get going if you can," I said, and he quieted down.

Uncle Matteo had stood up in the meantime. "Now you're playing games, both of you," he said. "But I know your kind. You'll throw a stone and pretend it wasn't you. Like during the elections when you let them beat me black and blue. I bet you were the ones who put them up to it!"

I nearly let Berto finish him off at that point, but the old man, without taking time to dust off his trousers, had turned back to the harvesters and said, "Go on, you two. Get back to work!"

"We don't want any trouble. We just came to work."

"Well, work then! You've been paid, haven't you!"

Which meant he had foreseen something like this; otherwise he wouldn't have been caught dead paying in advance!

"Stop now," I called out to them, "or you'll be in for it!"

I grabbed Berto, shoved the scythe into his hand, and told my son, my wife, and my sister-in-law to take their tools and follow me to the other side of the field, where the wheat was still untouched. I lined them up and called to the workers, "All right, let's work! Let's see how far you get and how far we get! We'll see who's better!"

A nervous tremor ran through my family; they raised their heads and laughed and later began to sing, working without letup. It seemed the most beautiful day of our lives. Nita and my little nephew marched behind us; all by themselves they had begun to glean. We felt neither heat nor hunger nor thirst. My wife removed the sheaves I cut, my sister-in-law removed Berto's, and every so often they wiped the sweat from our brows with their shirtsleeves and smiled at us.

My long-legged son was always a step ahead of us.

By noon we had harvested an acre; only stubble and carefully stacked piles of tied sheaves lay behind us. Ahead, between what the two day workers had cut and what little was left to cut, there was no more than about three-fourths of an acre.

"Enough!" I called out. "We'll leave the rest to the birds. Or to you, Uncle Matteo, if you want it!"

But he had sprawled out under the cherry tree, and at the sound of my words he turned toward the hedge and began to sob, his shoulders shaking violently. There he lay like a derelict robbed of his children, his wife, his home, his dearest possession. But I experienced no compassion: the land I felt was mine gave me strength, as did the grain I had just cut—it is so yellow at that instant, fairly bursting with the sun. I even called out to him, "We'll be using Gelmo's threshing machine too!"

And so it was. Instead of using the Vardizza thresher, as we had every year since the two old men had quarreled, we asked Gelmo to come up the hill. Lunching under the old man's oak tree and giving orders to his men, Gelmo felt the weight of ten years lift from his shoulders.

■ □ ■ □ ■

VIII

WORD SPREAD: THE REAPERS HAD TALKED. MANY THOUGHT WE were right. People stopped me and said, "You did what needed to be done. You harvested what was yours. Your uncle's never been an honest man." "And we thought you were in perfect harmony," others said. "No, he shouldn't have done it. You're his own flesh and blood. Here he is, about to kick the bucket, and you've been working for him forever!"

Then there were those who shrugged their shoulders and continued on their way, former landowners mostly, linked by the same rules as my uncle, and getting ready to set off for Trieste.

Some of the reactions annoyed me. Suddenly Franjo was buying me drinks; one of the Chersa boys started saying hello again; Rozzan forgot how to speak to me and would nudge his companions and stop talking as soon as he saw me; Giovanni Bože seemed friendlier than before.

But I wasn't jumping for joy. I knew that, if anything, all this attention took me a step backward. I didn't care about the harvest. I wanted what was mine; I wanted the land. And the old man was getting even meaner and maybe now would give up nothing. Being selfish was one thing, but stubbornness and hatred would take things further than simple self-interest. Hadn't we seen cases of people before the war who, while not letting a greedy uncle tell them their business, had lost all their land in the courts? So in spite of the support, I grew sadder by the day.

Once, sulfuring the Bussía vines that border the Rossis' in Pizzudo, I found myself eating lunch with the eldest Rossi brother in the path between our two properties. Since he had always been in favor of the Free Territory, I asked him what he thought I ought to do.

"See Vanja. He can do anything. He's the party secretary."

"I've already been to the judge."

"It's not the same. The party's what gets things going. Hear me out."

I did, and the next day I was in Buje again.

Vanja was a tall, blond man from near Fiume. He listened, smiling and nodding from time to time. Then he picked up the telephone, asked for the judge, and said, "One of the Koslović brothers from Materada is here to see me."

He said no more, listening for a long time while someone spoke on the other end of the line. At last he said, "*Zdravo*"— Bye—and hung up, his face dark. "Are you in the party?" he asked, using the informal form of *you*.

When I said no, he went back to the formal form.

"So what do you think? Aren't you satisfied with getting the fruits of the harvest and letting him keep his papers?"

He wasn't a person to whom I could say, "I want what's mine," so I answered, "Why should he have title to the land when he doesn't own it?"

"What does that matter to you? He has title to the land, yes, but you'll work it, harvest it every year."

"And what will I leave to my children one day?"

"Don't worry about your children. The People's State will take care of them. It takes care of everyone."

"Sorry, but I'd rather take care of them myself. At least as long as I'm alive."

Serious as he was, he broke into laughter, saying, "You peasants are all alike!" and started pacing the room in long strides. Then he looked at me suddenly and asked, "Supposing I found you an allotment bigger and more beautiful than the one your uncle owns, at Dàila for instance or in the Quieto valley, would you go and farm that?"

I could tell he was studying me. "Who owns the allotment?"

"The People's State."

"I understand. But who did it belong to before?"

"A landlord who left it, decided he'd rather go off to Italy."

I thought for a moment and said dryly, "No, I wouldn't."

"Why not?"

"Because one day it might not be mine anymore."

"So you have that little faith in us? You believe we, too, will fall and disappear?"

He was smiling.

I rearranged myself in my chair and answered, "Listen, Vanja. I don't know what you're aiming at, and I don't know very much about politics, but if you want my opinion, well, I'll tell you straight out. For as long as I can remember, we've had outsiders here, first the Austrians, then the Italians, then the Germans, and now you. They all left, and they were stronger than you. I myself saw the eagle fall, then the fasces and the swastika. Why shouldn't the hammer and sickle fall one day too?"

Again he laughed and slapped me on the shoulder. "You're a clever one, Koslović. But don't go saying such things to anyone else. You don't understand yet." He paused a moment and added, "If we give you the land, would you join the *skupčina*?"

"No, I don't think so."

He stopped in the middle of the room and looked at me stealthily. "If we didn't, would you, too, opt for Italy?"

That left me breathless, but I recovered quickly, and it was my turn to find his weak spot (something he believed I couldn't have understood): "If you give me the land, you won't be doing me a favor. You'll just be giving me what's mine. Doing justice. Don't we see all over the walls: '*Tudje nećemo, svoje ne damo*' [What is others' we do not want, what is ours we shall not give]?"

He slapped me on the shoulder again and said, "You're not one to get flustered, Koslović."

I got up to leave, but he stopped me. "Are you going to Giurizzani?" He asked. "Wait. I'll give you a ride."

It was a beautiful black Mercedes.

The driver stopped in front of Gelmo's, and I didn't know how to manage getting out without being seen by all those people talking and laughing under the mulberry tree. But while I was fumbling for the door handle, Vanja said, "Hold on. I can take you all the way home."

So he let me off in front of our elm and continued on toward Grotta, where, I assumed, he would be going to consult with Franjo.

That evening they came in through the cane gate, like the others had during the elections. Giovanni Bože was with the two of them and a man I didn't know from the Domestic Affairs Office. The dog was barking; it wanted to attack them, eat them up, but they didn't pay any attention, not like the policeman who had come from the city and called out he wouldn't take another step if we didn't chain up the dog. You could tell they'd been around dogs, at night, in the woods, that in a sense they were villagers like us.

I took them into the kitchen and had them sit down. They asked for Uncle Matteo, and Oliva ran upstairs to call him. In the meantime, Vanja talked in Croatian with my daughter, and she answered well because she had been in school for two years. Franjo and Giovanni talked to Berto, then turned to tell me in our local Croat dialect, which the other two didn't understand, to keep quiet and let them do the talking.

My uncle opened the stairway door and stood still on the top step. "Good evening, gentlemen," he said. "What's new?"

Everyone stood up.

"Come down," said Vanja. "We've got something to tell you."

But he was mistrustful and looked from one face to another. "I can hear very well from here. Besides, with the exception of these four fine gentlemen, I don't know who you are or why I should have to answer your questions."

"Stop putting on airs, gramps," said the man from the Domestic Affairs Office.

Then Franjo stepped in, going upstairs to him and saying, "There's nothing wrong, Uncle Tio. We're just here to have a talk." And he dragged him down into the kitchen.

Everyone was silent and tense. Glancing at the women and children watching the scene with mouths agape, I opened the door to the dining room.

"If you have anything to say to one another," I said, "go in there."

"No, no," Vanja objected, taking my brother's arm, "you come too."

The conversation began.

"Why don't you want to leave the land to your nephews?" asked Vanja.

"I've already explained everything to the judge. I don't recognize your authority to make me answer your questions."

The Domestic Affairs officer sprang up. "Be careful what you're saying," he said, "or you'll find out who we are."

But he was playing a part, it was clear, like scolding a baby just to scare it. I even noticed Vanja wink at him as if to say he'd gone far enough. I thought how many of us had been scared shitless during the past ten years in situations like this or for less even, but Uncle Matteo found the strength to plead his case.

"You come into my home, attack me as if I were a criminal, and I'm an old Croat. I was Croatian before you boys. I carried our flag with stones whizzing past my ears before you were born."

He was clearly moved by his own words, and Vanja softened up a bit. "It's nothing serious, Tio," he said. "You know how it is when people talk. Things get a little heated, and you say more than you mean. Let's be friends, all right? All we want to know is why you refuse to leave a little land to your nephews."

The old man pretended to wipe away a tear, but he was only playing for time.

"Others came and took the land I left them. Ask anyone. I always did right by them, and I bought them a nice piece of land. And now look what they've done. Attacked me, in case you didn't know, and beat me. What is it they want from me? Tell them to try and get the land back from the people who stole it from them."

"Excuse me," said Vanja, his voice kind, "but we were the ones who stole their land."

"Then give it back to them and leave me in peace."

The two leaders exchanged a glance. Then the Domestic Affairs officer said quietly, "Why you old rascal. If the People's State took it, it means you had too much. Now the wrong's been righted, and there's an end to it. But you must divide your land, and if you refuse, we're ready to take you with us."

"But why? What have I done to deserve this?"

"You've exploited them all these years. You're a reactionary *kulak;* we kill all *kulaks.* Tell me," he said, turning to the two of us, "has he given you half the money he's been salting away?"

"He hasn't given us a thing!" said Berto.

"How can you say that?" Uncle Matteo shouted. "Who was it that clothed and fed your wives and children when you went away to fight with the Italians?"

"One moment please," said one of the two leaders. "What about the money? Where did you put the money? We'd like to see the money you made from other people's labor!"

"There's no money here," he answered.

"That's for sure," cried Berto. "He sent it all to Trieste!"

My arms fell limp at my sides. "What are you saying?" I asked.

"Quiet you," said Vanja. "We want to see the money you've accumulated all these years. Is it true you sent it to Trieste? You'd better tell us everything, or you're coming with us!"

"You profiteer!" the Domestic Affairs officer yelled.

But the old man had stood up and slipped into the kitchen. He grabbed the scythe from the table and made for the stairs, slamming the door behind him and calling, "If you want me, come and get me!" Then he ran up and locked himself in his room.

The others were in the kitchen by then, and I had placed myself at the foot of the stairs to prevent them from going up. But it was all a joke, as I said. They had just wanted to frighten him.

They took their seats and began banging their fists violently on the table and calling out so he could hear, winking at one another all the while.

"Our graveyards aren't full yet!" they cried. And "There's still room in our jails!"

"That's enough now," I said. "This isn't what I wanted. Who asked you to come?"

"Take it easy, you," said the Domestic Affairs officer; and the two of them started laughing, like it was a boyish prank. Then Franjo began to laugh, but without humor, like a real bastard.

My wife took the wailing baby into her arms and came over to us. She turned to us men and to all the men on earth, who are forever sowing quarrels and more quarrels, and said, "Wind this up once and for all, I beg you. Put an end to this mess, or else I don't know what might happen. We can't live like this anymore. There's nothing but fighting and fear in our house and all because of the goddamn land. And here the children are hearing everything, all these evil doings, and. . . ."

She fell against the bench and started heaving sobs as long and quiet as dew. And I realized how little care we had shown for our wives and children to that day. I looked around the kitchen, saw our old fireplace, the benches, the pots and pans shining in their racks, and asked myself what these outsiders were doing here in our house. I realized how little interest they took in us, in our fate and our land; all they wanted was to settle an old score with Uncle Matteo; they hadn't been able to earlier because he had declared himself Croatian and so had forced them to settle accounts with others first. But now their chance had come—I'd given it to them myself—and they wanted to lord it over us one more time before everyone left for Italy. Everything fit their plans. I showed them to the door and said, "Thanks for all you tried to do for us, comrades."

And there, at the door open to all the countryside below, under the oak that made the sky still darker and the night still blacker, I stood alone and cursed that land forever.

Uncle Matteo waited until they had gone down to the road and came back into the kitchen.

"This is the last time we'll ever speak," he said. "I just want to tell you what bastards you are!"

My brother and I, exhausted, were sitting, one on a chair, the other on the bench, and we didn't have the courage to answer him. So he went on quickly, "So this is who I keep under my roof! A couple of spies! You even brought up the money in Trieste to get rid of me more quickly and enjoy the fruits of my labor! That's the 'family' I've kept in my house. Who knows how long you've been wronging me in secret! You're the ones who had me beaten during the elections!"

Finally I found the strength to stop him. "What are you talking about? I grabbed a pitchfork to defend you."

"I know your game. You grabbed it when they'd all but finished me off, when I was sprawled out on the ground, nearly choking in my own blood! Who was it left the gate open? Who showed them the way?"

I left him to babble and went back into the open, under the oak, in the dark of the deep night. And there I cursed again that land forever. I pictured every field one by one, every hedge, every plant, every furrow, and I cursed them, cursed them all. May they never more give fruit or seed; may hail fall on them year after year; may they wither like the hands of the dead.

I X

ONE EVENING A FEW DAYS LATER, FRANJO SENT WORD THAT I was to report to the school in Giurizzani. It was nine P.M. when I entered the hall where I had finished elementary school thirty years before.

After many months of calm and silence, they were holding—and on my account—one of those secret meetings that had decided the fate of so many people. It was the last one, I think, they would ever have in Giurizzani.

Everything was set up like I'd pictured it a thousand times: behind the table, where Mr. Romeo had once sat, Franjo was sitting, along with Giovanni Bože, Ciano, the kolkhoz president, and the youngest Chersa boy, who had recently started saying hello to me again. Rozzan was sitting on the ground; he had no business being there; he was just passing by and in everyone's way. Toni Lessio was sitting on the first bench—even if they'd dismissed him three years before—and Toni Jurisević and Nini Gazde, who were known as old warriors, though in reality they hadn't ever seen a gun other than a hunting rifle. The two benches behind them were occupied by the so-called new forces: sons who'd been off to study and the hungry crowd that knew only how to yell and did so more out of faith than reason.

They all stood up as I entered. They were friendly and called me by my first name. They had me come forward between the table and the school benches, where those big strong men were seated now as if they were schoolboys again. Franjo was the first to take the floor. It should be noted that when he spoke in public, he imitated the leaders who came to the Dom—his tone was like Vanja's, he waved his hands and slammed his fist like Medizza—but between one and the other, there was still something left of our gardens and our stables, and what he said went something like this:

"Franz, pal, we've called you here among us to resolve once and for all the question that is so close to your heart and that we, as good comrades watching over the interests of the working people, must resolve in common. A great injustice has been done you. And by whom? Somebody who thinks he can lay down the law in our land, who is still intent on sucking the blood from the poor and doesn't realize times have changed and that the workers, once so cruelly oppressed, can now lift up their heads and say, 'Enough!'"

He pounded his fist loudly on the table, and everyone applauded.

Stupefied, I watched and wondered how he had grown so clever in so short a time.

"But you (and your family and your brother's family) have always been one of us. In the terrible years of fascism when we could not speak our language, and during the glorious Battle for Liberation, when you, too, like most sound people of Materada, gave what you could in your poverty. You have committed only one crime, and you know it better than I do, since I've told you more than once, namely, that you wavered before taking the right path, that you didn't tell us what your true position was, that, free man that you are, you didn't accuse the man who was keeping you and your family in slavery. But we have waited for you. And today, just when reactionary forces have returned to make propaganda and speak ill of Yugoslavia, and people are going so far as to leave for an Italy that has never done us anything but evil, we're especially pleased that you have been able to see things right on your own and raise your head and shout, 'Enough!'"

Again everybody applauded, even louder. The opening remarks thus completed, it was time for the facts. Franjo changed his tone and began speaking quickly. "Comrade Vanja has been here with us and other comrades too. They said this thing must be resolved, that it's shameful to have someone here among us still seeking justice. And we are the first to admit it." He turned to the public and asked, "What do you think?"

"Yeah! That's right! Down with profiteers! Death to reactionary forces!"

"We've thought things over for a long time. There's just one way out. And you have to help us and help yourself at the same time. Your uncle won't hear of giving you the land. He'll never give it to you. And we can't take it from him because his papers are in order, even if—as we all know too well—it's nothing but a fraud. But now, Franz, we want you to show up the fraud, to tell the whole truth publicly: how your uncle took possession of the inheritance from your father, how he vainly promised you this and that and meanwhile pocketed everything himself, sending it all to Trieste, in a boat or however, I don't know."

I froze.

"I don't understand," I said, my voice shaking.

"You will," he said and asked Giovanni Bože to pass him his briefcase.

He took out a sheet of typewritten paper.

"There's only one way to get back the land, and it's the most just. Your uncle will have to be condemned. So a suit will have to be drawn up to reexamine his property or, rather, his fraud. Here," he said.

The paper contained new accusations against my uncle, and everything seemed to be written in my name. I turned it over in my hands and asked, "Who wrote this?"

"We did. In your best interests."

"You were wrong. I'm not signing."

They jumped up as if an electric current had gone through them. "What's the meaning of this? Why? We demand an explanation!"

"Because what you've written here is false."

"How can you say that?" yelled Franjo.

"It's false, and you ought to be ashamed of yourselves."

Franjo came right up under my nose with his treacherous little eyes.

"I had you pegged, so we deliberately interrogated your brother first!"

I was furious, "Why do you believe my brother? He's no man."

"No, you're no man. You're the one who wants to hide the truth now!" He turned to his comrades and said, "See? What did I tell you? See who we're dealing with? He beats his fist on the table, but he's really scared shitless!"

They were all laughing behind my back except Giovanni Bože. I could see he wanted to help me.

"These are lies," I said. "I'm not signing."

Franjo looked like someone possessed.

"Look at him," he yelled. "A brave man!"

There was more laughter, but in the moment of quiet that followed I asked, "You mean you're a brave man?"

Silence.

"You who sent Gioachin to denounce Nando to the judges?"

"Listen to him!" he said before I could finish. "And we thought he was one of us!"

"I never asked to be."

"Quiet, sellout!" Chersa roared.

The men on the back benches started banging their fists and stomping their feet, making a hellish racket. I stared at them all with wide eyes, hardly believing they had changed so in a few seconds, the hands then open and applauding now closed into so many menacing fists.

"What do you do with men like him?" Franjo asked. And the others answered, "Hang them!"

Aside from Giovanni Bože, only Rozzan didn't know what to do. His face was all red, and his eyes begged pity from me yet hated me too for not being like the others.

"What about you, Rozzan?" Franjo asked. "What do you say?"

"About what?" Rozzan asked in turn. But the men thought he had done it on purpose, to make fun of me, and they burst into laughter again.

"What do you think needs to be done with people like him?"

He looked at me, shrugged his shoulders, and said, "It takes patience."

Everyone laughed at his patience. Then Chersa said, "People like him are worse than bosses. They'll always be slaves."

"Wait a second," somebody else said, "he's no slave. He wanted to take over his uncle's place and be boss himself!"

"And now they'll go off to Trieste to tell the monks how awful the life is here!"

"Right," said Chersa, my uncle's ex–hired man, "and good riddance! Go ahead! What are you waiting for? Go and let the Italians screw your wife and they'll put up a monument to you!"

They were laughing again, and I just stood there with that sheet of paper in my hand. So I tore it up, tore it into a thousand pieces, and said, "You're the worst pack of worms to crawl the earth. Who put you in charge anyway, you poor sheep? All you want is to copy the big shots; you don't know how to talk for yourselves. Oh, you do know how to look after your own interests, that you know, and how to get rid of anyone who stumbles into your path. You've still got manure on your hands, and now it's all over your armchairs. Real workers know enough to wash their hands after work. But what's dirty stays dirty. Maybe stupid Chersa here got some land from my uncle. Maybe that's why he's talking and laughing and raising his voice and presuming to judge me! You ought to be ashamed of yourselves, all of you! You're the reason people are leaving in droves."

I hurled the pieces of paper to the ground, and they went as far as Chersa, who stood up and struck me.

"Sellout!" he cried.

I took three steps back, wiped the swelling lip, and said softly, "I was slapped once before twenty years ago. You all know it. This time it was much harder."

I left the room with all of them following me in silence with their eyes. I felt free and content in a way. Getting slapped doesn't hurt in some instances: you feel you no longer owe anything to anybody. All I wanted was to get drunk. My legs seemed to be taking me to the Dom, but I eventually veered off in the direction of Gelmo's.

It was Saturday. Several people were playing cards at two tables; others formed small groups at the counter and in the corner where I had talked with Rozzan during the Easter feast.

Everyone looked up as I entered, but nobody said hello. I saw my brother sitting alone at a table and, from the way he was squirming off by himself I could tell he'd failed to join one of the groups and ended up getting drunk by himself.

"Good evening," I said loudly.

Silence. Then, "Evening," said Milio.

They changed the subject as I approached the counter and looked at me suspiciously. I was at a loss and tried to keep my swollen lip hidden. "How are things, little hunchback?" I asked Milio.

"The weather's fine, just fine," he said quickly.

I asked Italo for a beer. "We're out of beer," he answered.

At that I raised my voice: "And what are these gentlemen drinking? It looks like beer to me."

"It is, but there's no more left. I gave the last bottle to Bortolo."

But by then Gelmo had rushed over, solicitous and joking. "No beer? What do you mean? There's always beer for friends."

He pulled out a bottle from the sideboard from his reserve for people he either trusted or suspected. Italo was furious. "You blame me! You're the one who ordered me not to serve any more!"

But Gelmo only laughed, baring his false teeth and calling Italo an idiot. He explained to me that only nine cases had been delivered because the truck coming from Ljubljana got unloaded at Umago, in Punta, where there were lots of tourists of all types and stripes—Italians, French, Austrians, Serbs, and Americans, and the devil and his mother, but that for friends he always put a few bottles aside.

I didn't know whether to thank him or not because I knew very well who the friends he had in mind were, so I said, "Then keep it for your closest friends, and give me a quarter-liter of wine."

But he acted as if he were offended and wanted nothing more than to open the bottle for me.

I drank it in peace, though I could see Milio watching me out of the corner of his eye. Then I heard him say loudly, so I could hear, "Yes, Bortolo, they're going back to those tough early years here. Forty-five, forty-six, forty-seven, forty-eight, forty-nine . . ."

"'Fifty," I said, and when they failed to respond I added, "Didn't they hold elections in fifty?"

He was still rude to me and said, without looking at me, "That was something different. They were outsiders, not our own." And as if he'd made some great statement—and also not to spoil the effect by sticking around—he said good-bye to the others and left, banging the door.

Poldo left too, along with two others, and I thought how wrong they were about me and about themselves. They had all done as they pleased during the years Milio had listed, and when everyone was grabbing they, too, had been ready to grab as much from the new idea as would further their own interests. Poldo, who was always going to church to beat his breast and demonstrate against the regime and who worked half the land of a sister-in-law who lived in Trieste, had harvested the whole crop from '45 on and hadn't let her have a bag of flour to fry herself a fish in.

I called my brother. "Let's get going," I said. "Tomorrow morning we've got to plow the stubble under."

We started off for home. Once past the "lake," where they bring livestock for watering, we had only the dark, empty road before us. "Well, what did you do?" I said, stopping.

"Nothing," he said, his voice trembling. He was expecting it. "What do you mean?"

"You can still ask me that? You bastard! Who told you to talk?"

I grazed his neck with my fist. He shielded himself with his hands, and I kicked him once, then again, until he turned to fight back. Then I punched him in the face and said, "Let this be a lesson to you."

I made him get up and walked at several paces behind him, keeping a close eye on him all the way home.

■ □ ■ □ ■

X

WHAT WAS THERE TO DO NOW? ONE SIDE WAS AGAINST ME AND so was the other, I didn't have the land but still worked it, and there wasn't any money left in the house. By taking the little bit my wife had made from the eggs and milk, I managed to scrape together fifty thousand dinars to pay for the threshing, and went off to Gelmo's.

Along the way I thought things over: I've tried every way possible to get justice, but in vain; so let's go to the old school, tried and true; it won't let me down.

"Listen, Gelmo," I said. "I've come to give you the threshing money but also to get your advice."

Seeing the money, he wasn't suspicious anymore, and despite his fear and wariness, he was happy at heart to be thought of as a man of the world, an old-time landowner, and to be asked his opinion.

He had me sit down in the dining room.

"Here's how things stand," I said. "I've done everything possible to get back the land: I've asked, I've begged, I've humiliated myself and shouted. I tried playing nice with my uncle and playing rough. None of it has done any good. I'm taking a step back every day. At first he might have let me take something, but now I'm sure he wouldn't give me a vegetable garden. What should I do? You tell me. You've got more experience."

"Is he at least ready to discuss things? What does he say when you give him your reasons?"

"He understands only his own."

"I see."

"Then there's only one way to behave," he said, brushing some crumbs from the table.

He raised his head and fixed me with his cunning eyes. "Don't pay any attention to him. Do everything as if he didn't exist. Don't even talk to him. Pretend there's nothing going on."

"What do you mean?"

He nearly lost his temper: men of the world were supposed to come to understandings at a glance. "Christ," he said, "don't you see? You've got to act like the boss. You've got stock in the barn? Wine in the cellar? Grain in the loft? Okay, sell it. Go about your business. You'll see how the old man comes running after you. And let him, out of spite."

"That's what you think?"

"There's no other way," he said, getting up. Then he leaned over and spoke into my ear, pointing to the room: "It was right here your uncle betrayed me. Been fifteen years now. And I thought he was my friend. But you can't treat him like a man, let alone a friend. You've got to use his ways and do him over in business. You did the right thing to harvest the wheat. Now sell it."

As the next day was dawning, I put on clean trousers and a freshly ironed shirt and went into the barn and tied the calf by its horns. I hadn't slept all night, just as I imagined my uncle hadn't slept fifteen years before, after coming home from Gelmo's. Now he was awake though: I could hear him banging on something upstairs.

When he heard the calf crying and its mother calling it from inside the barn, he leaned out of the window and said, "Hey, where are going?"

But I didn't answer him and, using a staff I'd made out of a branch from the oak, I drove the calf outside the cane gate. I heard the old man shouting, "Stop! Where are you going? What's got into you?" as I kept straight on and almost felt like laughing.

When I got to the road in front of the elm, I could see him jumping over the ditches, holding his trousers with one hand and waving his cane, making signs for me to stop, with the other.

I took the shortest road, through Sterpín, neither quickening nor slowing my pace, as if he didn't exist. But before I got to Milio's vines he'd caught up. "What's going on?" he said. "What's the story?"

I held my tongue, and he kept raising his voice. "Pretending to be deaf? Answer me. I asked you where you're taking the calf! Look here now. Are you going to tell me or what?"

I was walking so fast he was barely able to keep up, and he still had to fasten his trousers. I had to force myself not to laugh at that point. Gelmo had really guessed right. I was happy to be walking through the green with the calf that had by then forgotten its stall and was running as if I were taking it to pasture or to a fair, and with the sun coming up behind Buje, warming the nape of my neck.

"You going to stop, you bastard?" Uncle Matteo cried in a hoarse voice. "What do you think you're doing? I could go to the Militia and denounce you, you know that? How can you take something that's not yours?"

I just let him talk, but by the time we reached the Sterpín houses, he had to answer the greetings of the people who saw us, so he decided to change his strategy.

"Look at him, everybody!" he said more gently. "Have you gone crazy, Francesco? You won't even answer me? Look what you're doing to your old uncle! Making him run like a kid!"

Then he laughed a pitiful laugh. "Really, you rascal! We're no youngsters anymore, you and me. Maybe you forgot I'm nearly seventy?!"

But I just blew my nose and goaded the animal with the leaves at the end of the branch.

At Giurizzani I took the road for Umago. The old man realized I was going to the slaughterhouse and, because there were lots of people watching us by then, he took another tack. There was a big truck from Umago parked in front of

Bortolo's, and my uncle said hello to the people there and asked, "What's this truck doing in Giurizzani?"

"Bortolo's application's been approved. He's leaving for Trieste."

"Poor guy. Going away and leaving everything. My, my, the world really is all mixed up!"

Huffing and puffing through his thick mustache, he buttoned up his trousers, and even though nobody responded he went on. "Yes, we're going to the slaughterhouse. What do you expect? There are times when you've got to sell something off. There wasn't much hay this year. All that rain."

He snickered, wagging his head and once even giving me a wink. "Bortolo's leaving," he said, as though taking me into his confidence, "and God go with him! He can count on his wife's pension: she's a teacher. And then his kids, they're studying, they'll bring in something. No, don't worry, they know what they're doing."

I began to wonder whether he really had gone crazy. Near Petrovia he said, "I don't want to interfere, Francesco. Just don't let them cheat you on the weight. And don't give in on the price either, because you won't find meat like this every day." And he gave the calf's haunch a firm slap.

A truck passed by, and I was afraid the animal would spook, since it hadn't ever been out of its stall before. But the old man came to my aid, stepping in front of the calf, and, stroking its forehead, driving it over to the hedge.

The slaughterhouse had just one steer to be killed, so the calf was like a gift.

"Hello, gents!" said my uncle, raising his cane. "Just look what a fine animal we've brought you. You're lucky we had that cold spell, or you'd have had to wait a long time for a nice one like this! So, what will you give me for it?"

I realized he was trying to cheat me, so I stepped in immediately.

"You deal with me," I said. "This man has nothing to do with the calf."

A half-argument followed. I talked to the butchers; he talked to me.

"Make up your minds, you two," said the head butcher. "Whose name do we write on the receipt?"

"Francesco Koslović."

"*Matteo* Koslović!"

"Francesco!!"

"Matteo!!! It's my calf; you deal with me. He stole it!"

But they believed me more because I wasn't so worked up. "If he stole it," they said to him, "go to the Militia and turn him in."

He did so, and a little later they sent for me. I explained the situation to the *kommandir,* and he phoned Giurizzani. After talking directly to Giovanni Bože, he said to my uncle, "You've got no claim on the calf. The receipt goes to your nephew." And he issued me a piece of paper.

By the time I returned to the slaughterhouse, the animal was hanging from a spike, the blood dripping from its nose.

"So who was right?" asked the head butcher.

I showed him the paper. My uncle was fuming. "It's got nothing to do with us; believe me," he said. "It's the women. You know how they are, women. We'll settle things between us, Francesco, the way we always do."

But his eyes betrayed him, and when they wrote my name on the receipt and afterward, when I withdrew the money from the bank, I could have sworn he was on the brink of tears.

The return trip was exactly the reverse of the trip there. At first he thought he could get on my good side, but then he lost his temper and took to threatening me. I left him at Giurizzani insulting me in front of a crowd.

I shrugged my shoulders and went off to buy some tobacco.

The truck in front of Bortolo's house was ready to go, packed full of furniture, crates, sacks, and cages with hens inside.

I stopped to watch, a little away from the others.

Milio was on top of the heap, calling for a handful of straw to put under the mirror from the master bedroom. His two sons—and boys from families thinking of leaving, if they hadn't already submitted their applications—were helping him from below.

The customs official from Umago, a Serb named Branko, was examining each item, piece by piece. Before the oil was loaded, he cut a long stick with his pocketknife and dipped it into the barrel.

All the people from the village were standing there looking on, the women on one side, the men on the other, the children at their feet.

Rather than put his money into the bank in Capodistria, Bortolo had preferred to spend it all: he was going around in a new suit, offering drinks to all the men and smiling at the women with the new false teeth he'd put in that morning and hadn't got used to yet, talking with his lips tight, as if he had a pair of tongs in his mouth.

There was one last big chest to hoist. It was covered with dust and spiderwebs and was more beautiful than the newer ones, still white from planed, unvarnished wood. You could see it had come from elsewhere, not from our parts, and I remembered it was the trunk the teacher, Miss Lina, had brought from Italy for her trousseau. How many years had passed since then? I could hear her talking to a woman in her soft voice, see her caressing one of her pupils, and I wondered if she'd ever thought that after living a life in our parts she and her husband and grown children would have to pull down her old wedding trunk from the attic.

Milio shouted that he'd finished, the customs man gave a once-over glance, and the driver climbed into the cab to start the engine. It was like when they carry the deceased from the house and the band begins to play.

The women, crying, called out, "Good-bye, Miss Lina. You were always kind to us. You brought up our kids."

The old couple was crying too and kissing everyone, one by one. It was something to see two elderly people crying without a death in the family, without the doctor in their house or their fields destroyed by hail, dressed in their Sunday best and going where they had long yearned to go.

They came up to me too and kissed me, and I wished them well and waved, and dried a tear in secret.

The first truck was leaving from Giurizzani. It left us sad and shrouded in the smoke and stench it poured out behind.

For a while the people stood there confused. Then each, wiping his eyes, went off on his own, still unsettled.

I set out for the Dom for tobacco. I felt I had to run, to hurry, as if I'd been wasting time, though I couldn't explain why.

XI

BORTOLO'S DEPARTURE FROM GIURIZZANI WAS LIKE WHEN A sheep finds an opening in a hedge and all the others go crazy trying to rush through after it.

The towns of Istria were emptying day by day, especially the ones on the coast, and it was normal for us to see the same trucks reeling under pitiful heaps, leaving Umago and Buje for Trieste. But nobody thought the countryside would start to move too.

For a while people went about it in secret, and suddenly the bomb exploded: everybody was leaving. One evening you'd be talking to a friend at the tavern—you didn't talk about anything else then—and the guy who'd always said, "I don't mind dying, but in my own house," seemed different, hesitant, and the next morning you learned he'd gone to Umago to hand in his application. It was like a hailstorm. A father-in-law wouldn't leave if his daughter wasn't going; the son-in-law found he had three or four against him and, his back against the wall, had to give in; and then even his parents and brothers ended up leaving.

At the funeral of old Rosso from Pizzudo you could calculate that about half the population had gone. Waiting under the acacias for the Croatian priest from Buje, we did nothing but recount the latest news and argue, each one insisting on his own view of things. There hadn't ever been so many people at a funeral, and very few went up to throw holy water on the poor dead man; not even the women were crying. Some people were waiting for the truck to arrive; some were getting their applications ready; some were waiting to see what others would do and in the meantime listening in a little here, a little there to get a better grip on the situation. The first to start moving were those, like Bortolo, who had either children or work on the other side and who would have left anyway as soon as the barriers at the crossing point had been lifted. Then came those who'd done time or who'd always shown their antagonism and been deprived of identity cards and salt and clothing coupons. And finally those who had nothing but two good arms, people for whom working here or working there amounted to pretty much the same thing and who were just following the stream, especially since some could count on a brother or an uncle to send an invitation from America.

But that day at Pizzudo you heard people saying that even the big landowners from Fiorini were leaving. "Even they're packing up," it was said, "people who've never made less than twenty-five hundred gallons of wine a year, fifteen thousand pounds of wheat."

It meant there was nothing left here and only those mixed up in politics would be staying, or those too poor to leave their own troubles behind, the kind that would never do anything right. So the trucks kept coming to Giurizzani and other towns, and when they were too big to enter the courtyards the landlord would have to pull down the walls and trim the acacia branches.

They would pile up everything: old tables, woodworm-infested benches good only for winter evenings in Giurizzani, birdcages, vases planted with sweet basil, shiny glazed chamber pots, old documents and older tools. Then they'd leave, huffing and puffing, while we watched, bewildered yet moved. Venezia-Giulia Radio broadcast instructions: room and board was reserved for each person as well as a small subsidy for children and the elderly. Some groups were leaving for America, Australia, and Canada. Entry was open to everyone.

Within no time it was all the rage. You submitted an application, took your money to Capodistria or bought new clothes or furniture, and loaded up your things, giving one another a hand, and saying farewell once the driver started up the engine. And this among people who hadn't ever seen a church bell farther away than the one in Buje, or a wider street, or a higher mountain.

The people who stayed almost had to apologize for doing so. Even those known for cursing the hot summers and cold winters would open their arms and say, "See you on the other side," and then run behind a hedge or inside a barn to dry their tears.

Somebody would stop you and, without letting you get in a word, make a speech that invariably ended, "You can't stay here anymore," or "The best families are leaving, and who'll be left to talk to or do business with?" or "It's a tragedy: the first to have made the hole should have stopped it up!"

You could hardly wait to finish work, go down to the tavern, and meet like newlywed couples. And talk and talk: some had left from Sferchi, others from Villania and Cipiani and San Lorenzo and Vinella. There was even a guy who'd been in the Militia and another who'd been in the *skupčina*.

The customs official got stricter and stricter and passed only what was on the list. They said it was because at Fiorini he'd found nearly a million dinars in a bag of old rags. They allowed six hundred pounds of potatoes, a barrel of olive oil, a lot of flour and a pig and two cows per family. Butchers walked the checkpoint ready to make deals, their wallets filled with lire. Lire had become a rarity for us, something for luxury items only: vehicles, furs, perfumes. Dinars were crude, for buying farm tools, steers, and, if you were lucky, thick shoes and everyday clothes from the *zadruga*.

In the meantime, old stories came to the surface, stories of jealousies and betrayals, ancient ties long since forgotten. One person wouldn't leave unless another person did, and that other was tied to a third. Women almost always had their fingers in it: now they expected running water, and gas and electricity, and even a trolley waiting outside the door. And meanwhile you spent money because you had to use up those dinars that would turn to nothing in the bank in Capodistria. Gelmo said he never sold so much beer as that summer, and never so much wine, even though everyone's cellar was full. The young people had taken over: the old mostly prayed, trembling at the thought of being left alone in the house they'd built for their children; they let themselves take advice and then be led by the hand.

The local dance hall was transformed into a marketplace. How many marriages weren't arranged that summer in the Giurizzani Dom, even among children of seventeen or so and after one or two evenings. No one thought of land or dowries but of connections and prospects in Trieste. Grand days they were, in sum, for the old mothers. They felt they were getting married all over again and had leave to make a fresh start in new times. The poor farmer was even more discredited than before; the girls (the mothers) looked with fondness on the youngster who'd been clever enough to acquire a profession.

My wife told me she'd seen a girl (she didn't want to name her) change dance partners three times in one evening, parading each past her mother, and finally settle on a fourth, whom she had in fact married at town hall.

My sister-in-law said that as soon as Femia found out Lunardo was leaving, she tormented poor Sandro so much that she persuaded him to quit his prized job at the Umago Promet, submit an application, and put the tiny bit they owned on the list.

My son told us about how Silvano from Giurizzani had stopped the truck in front of the Dom because he realized he'd forgotten his goldfinch.

I told my daughter about how Mario Merischian's little boy didn't mind the others crying; he was happy to go ride in the tuk-tuk, and he blew up his lips and went "pum-pum-pum." And about how the Sitars' calf had jumped down from the truck and run back to its mother (they were taking her to the slaughterhouse) and about the trouble they'd had catching it again.

At that point my brother stopped me and said, "Hey, what about us?"

I shrugged and went back to playing with my daughter on my knees. But taking advantage of my silence, my wife said, "Everyone's made up their minds, and here you sit with your hands in your pockets. What have you got to show for it? Not the land, that's for sure! Do you want to go on serving the old man?"

My sister-in-law didn't let her finish. "They say the ones who get there first get the best treatment."

"The best young people are leaving," my son added without looking at me. "The ones staying behind are all married."

And my brother: "I'm not letting go of the land, but waiting here or waiting there, what's the difference?"

I shrugged again. "Well, you decide. I don't care. Do what you think is best. I'm going to Giurizzani."

And I went to see Old Man Nin.

XII

HE WAS SITTING UNDER THE MULBERRY TREE, SMOKING HIS putrid thorn-apple cigarette. He was a little irritable because they hadn't yet delivered the paper he liked to read straight through, shaking his head and commenting aloud, as if it had been written just for him and he wondered why they hadn't asked his opinion first.

He looked a little like Uncle Matteo, maybe because of the big mustache that poured down over his mouth, but next to my uncle he was a mountain, and he had kind eyes behind his glasses, a jocular way about him, and a carpenter's pencil tucked behind his ear, even though he hadn't used it for a long time except to make himself look good.

"Hello, Old Nin. How're you doing?"

He raised his head and sent me a look like a man past caring, though you could see him watching you behind it. Still mute, he indicated the cigarette with his eyes, as if to ask whether I could stand the stench. Then he looked around for a place for me to sit, and failing to find one, thundered in the direction of his little house, "A chair! A chair! A chair!"

Auntie Mena stuck her face out of the little window, her pointed, dark face that always looked like it'd been rummaging in the coffee grounds, and asked, "What do you need?"

"A chair! A chair! A chair!"

She responded by mumbling something and slamming down the shades.

I was about to start talking, but he stopped me with his hand and stayed like that until the woman, still mumbling, opened the door and shuffled out onto the threshing floor, pushing a chair, which she left a few feet away from him. He lowered his hand and waved it a couple of times loosely to let her know he wanted the chair closer.

Mena dragged it up to him and plopped it down right under his big nose. And while she stood there, stooped, fearing he might say something harsh, Old Man Nin took two fingers and touched her thin flesh among the thousand folds of her black, shiny dress. Then he looked away, pretending to be just passing by, not wanting to interfere, and she jumped back two steps and raised her fist and yelled, "Old swine!" as forcefully as she could. But she was in on it, she was, you could see: she yelled just because somebody else was there. That meant they had moments when they could touch each other freely, and even as she yelled, she was enjoying herself a little, the dark of her chin and upper lip laughing.

Old Man Nin, indulgent and superior, let her go on, knowing very well what was behind her yelling. Then, "Out!" he said sternly, waving his hand to make her stop, like an old piece of music that he, during his life as a bassist, had heard too many times. But she didn't give in, and on her way back into the house, which seemed built just for her, she warned she'd have the better of him next time.

As I sat down, Old Man Nin put his mustache to my ear and said, in a voice barely audible, "I know everything, Koslović. I expected you sooner."

"Then you're not against me like the others?"

He tapped his forehead with his index finger and said, "What do you think I've got in here?"

And he started to explain.

"In another time this thing would have gone through the hands of lawyers, who'd have eaten up your estate twice over, and you'd have lost anyway; or else you'd have gone at it with knives. Today you've harvested the wheat and sold the calf.

But that's not in your character. I know you wouldn't have done it if it wasn't for the regime and you hadn't seen others doing the same. Gelmo wouldn't have advised you to either. In another time you'd have gone around whining about your misfortunes, and nobody would have believed you and the youngsters would have thrown rocks at you."

"So I've made a mistake?"

"No. But you've done what they wanted. We've got no law, no order here: the first one up in the morning takes charge. You're obliged to do what they want, as a farm worker at least. As a landlord it's a different thing altogether."

"Well it's better than going around whining," I said. "What do you think of the regime?"

"Hard to say. It's a long road that'll lead God knows where, maybe backward. Who knows. To know you'd have to be born now." And he started to sing, "*No la me vol più ben,*" and then added, "Yes, you're too old, even if you are half my age. You'd have had to be born now."

"*La prega Dio che crepo e inveze stago ben.*"

I let him laugh and philosophize some more, and then asked, "So what should I do? I want the land, but the old man won't give in, and I'll lose it."

But all he did was laugh like a person whose affairs always come around. "See?" he said. "You're too old too. Yes, even you'd have had to be born now."

"Then what should I do?" I said more loudly.

He stopped laughing and shrugged. "Don't you see the others? What are the others doing? Why are you asking me?"

"So I should leave?"

"Why are you asking me?" he repeated, annoyed, as if the answer were as plain as the nose on my face. I decided to resort to cunning and asked, "So why aren't you leaving?"

But that made things worse. He started laughing hard, his toothless mouth wide open, ready to spout fat fist-sized toads, his wife looking on from the window, shaking her head as if he were an idiot.

"Should I leave?"

"Why ask me? Ask me about other things, about what it was like when I would play the bass at the dances and fairs or would let someone else play and go out to dance and spin ladies I could barely get my arms around, ladies of more than two hundred pounds!"

"All right," I said, spellbound. "What were they like?"

"They were beautiful times, my times!" And he wet and smoothed his mustache, as if he had once more become that dapper young bassist at the dances and the fairs. But it all sounded like the "good old days" that Milio had told me about at Gelmo's, so I said, "Not even you trust me anymore."

"Trust you? Everybody knows I took a punch at the elections, and I was nearly eighty at the time."

"No, you don't trust me."

At that he became serious and said, by way of conciliation, "Go then, Francesco. It's the lesser of two evils. Do like the others. Not all of them are right in leaving, in choosing the lesser evil. Many are, but others are just profiting from the situation. It's only natural. But you're one of the first."

"And what shall I do there?"

"Work, make another life for yourself, find another fortune."

"And what will they say there?"

"They'll give you a bed and a meal like the others."

"No, I asked what they'll *say*."

"What do you expect? All they care about is that you've left with the others."

"And people here?"

"What's it to you? What have they given you?"

"No, I mean our own people."

"I know. What do you care? Hand in the application and watch them scatter again. All they want is for you to confirm their decision. They want you to say or, better, prove they're doing the right thing by leaving."

Just then his son Italo appeared in the pathway through the acacias that led to Gelmo's. He had come to get a piece of bread. "Greetings to the lawyers and engineers," he said.

His father watched him go into the house and, shaking his head, said, "He's living in his own world, poor boy."

But when Italo reappeared at the door, nibbling at the bread, on his way back to Gelmo's, Old Man Nin saw him with a different pair of eyes. "He asked me, like you, if he should go," he said. "And I told him, 'Go ahead.' 'But what about you?' he asked. 'Don't think about me,' I said, 'cause all I need is some thorn-apple cigarettes and a couple of shovels of land. Go, ahead. Make your fortune.' 'But I don't have the heart to leave you and Mama alone,' he said. 'And when we're not around anymore?' I said. 'What'll you do when the wolves come? Who'll protect you? Who'll raise his cane to protect you from the wolves?'"

He seemed about to cry, but the tears didn't come. "Because I know he's not normal. He can't stay with them."

Only the elections brought a tear to his eyes. "Why'd they choose him? I had ten others. I wouldn't have cared if it'd been any of them. Why'd they have to hurt him, who's not like the others and was good to his neighbors and refused to leave me? Go ahead, I tell him, find your happiness."

He seemed to be talking to himself and despite his vigor I could hear the old man in him. To see him differently, as I wanted him to be, I changed the subject, "So, Old Nin, what were those times like?"

He smiled. Again he wet and smoothed his mustache and said, "Ask your uncle; ask that crook. I was on one side, he on the other. I the Italian, he the Croat. I with my flag and my people from the league, he with his flag and his *društvo* people. Austria allowed it. But those bastards accused us of setting fire to their Croatian school. No, I says, Your Honor, not that. You can say anything you like—that we'd thrown stones at them, that my brother Zorzi had relieved himself on their flag, that when we were coming back from Babici there were too many of

them and I had no choice but to signal a retreat and, before taking to my heels myself, I'd dropped my trousers and shown 'em
a thing or two, Your Honor—but not that we set fire to their
school. We're not from Serbia, not us. Find out for yourself.
Ask around. It was their women who burned the school down.
Did it when they were baking their bread. Not me, not my
people, Your Honor. And he took me at my word."

"So even then it was the same old story: Italians and Slavs
and Slavs and Italians?"

"But then it was all right!" he thundered. "That's the way
the world was. It was a way of having fun, not a play for
power. They danced the mazurka too. How many of our
youngsters dance it now?"

"You're right," I said. "The world's changed."

"For the worse!" he thundered again, and now I understood why at first he'd laughed and sang and said those things
I couldn't understand.

"There was a time men killed one another on the streets
for a woman. Now they kill out of a taste for killing, plus
they want to be right! But what reason did they have to kill
Silvano from Petrovia, stab him thirteen times on his way
back from the Buje fair where he'd played in the band—it
was the Nativity of the Virgin, the eighth of September in
'48, I'll never forget! And why? Oh, they came up with a
story about him being killed by the Triestines on account of
his having been a partisan, but four years later it came out it
was a guy from Castelvenere, from the People's Militia, and
just because he felt like it or got annoyed seeing Silvano playing and having a good time! Everybody was sorry, sure.
Everybody cried. The papers in Trieste went into all the par-
ticulars, the girls bringing flowers, the young men carrying
the coffin. But in the meantime he was gone. And who was
it, out of the thousands and thousands, who thought about
his clarinet, which he was coming back from the dance with?
Eh? It must have fallen to the ground, into the grass, while he
was being stabbed, and the next day they'd have found it

playing to him next to his head. But did you see it in the coffin, where they put his most precious things? No, you didn't. They didn't have the courage to let it be seen. Thirteen stab wounds, but in the end even they had respect or were afraid or ashamed of something."

I stared at him with my mouth open. In his agitation he was saying things I hadn't ever thought about. "But you wouldn't understand. You don't know what it means to play in a band and have your own instrument and take it home with you under your arm."

By then he had no more saliva—it was all over his mustache and around his lips—so he calmed down and said, "And now you ask me why people are leaving. Well, I'll tell you. Besides the money, which has a way of overpowering a man, there's one thing for sure: every one of them feels in his heart—even if the time hadn't been right for him to feel it until now—that in the end there has to be respect or fear or shame for something. Our chiefs would leave too; and so would their children who're off studying."

He shrugged his shoulders and spread his arms. "I don't know about tomorrow. I can't say. Maybe the world will change and there'll be no need to feel those things. I don't know. You'd have to be born now."

His throat had gone dry again, and with that pencil behind his ear, his glasses, and his thin neck, he looked like he'd just gulped down a plane full of wood shavings.

He glanced over at Mena's window, but he didn't want to call her: they had their own way of understanding each other. Old Man Nin played feeble, mumbling like a beggar, asking for a sip of water before going with God.

"What?" she shouted.

"Mhm . . . mhm . . ."

"Yes, but whaaat?" she asked again, coming to the window.

"Coffee! Coffee! Coffee!" he finally thundered.

"Well, come and get it if you like!" she shouted back, slamming down the shades.

Old Man Nin gave me a sly and satisfied wink, though I thought she'd had the better of him. And I saw him standing, much taller than me, strong and resolute, moving toward the little house made specially for her, Auntie Mena, where he could go only to subjugate and destroy or have himself cared for. As he lowered his head so as not to bump it, I thought, "There he goes, old man that he is, ready to shout and thrash, turn everything upside down, take her by the hips, and fling her on the bed."

I did in fact hear some pounding inside and shouting, and after a short silence, out he came with a big cup of black coffee and an even bigger piece of bread. He dropped it onto the table as if to show it was all you could get out of an old woman living by herself in a little house, then crumbled it into pieces, and dropped them into the cup, where they immediately began to swell up. When only a few white blotches remained, he started to devour it. He slurped at every spoonful and sucked like a double-hosed pump when the wine barrel is nearly empty.

At the same time he wanted to speak and lifted the empty spoon up to his forehead, but then went at it again, glancing at me quickly so I'd realize how busy he was for the time being.

His work completed, he put the cup aside and glanced with displeasure at the little pieces stuck to the inside. "Sell your uncle the tiles from the roof even," he said. "You won't ever get enough from him. But then leave. Think of your family. That's what counts."

But there was something else he'd wanted to tell me, and suddenly he remembered what it was. "I didn't think like poor Nando who, when he saw them going by, on May third of '45, stroked his chin and said, 'Good-bye homeland.' No, I'd always seen regular armies and professional troops who took to their heels at the first shot. Okay, you'll say, there was no point in fighting. The fate of Austria was sealed. One day I was shaving my commanding officer from Ljubljana, when he pointed to a sack and said, with his face all covered with soap, 'See that sack, Nin?' '*Ja*, Officer Sir.' 'If you fill it up, it stands; if you don't, it falls, right?' '*Ja*, Sir.' 'Well, that's how it'll be with Austria too. When it has no more to give its people to eat, it'll fall.' And that's how it was.

"So I saw soldiers who had run away (they couldn't have cared less about the war) and then these others: filthy, black with hunger, unrecognizable, one carrying a rifle, another a stake or a cane, marching toward Umago and, as if that weren't enough, happy and singing and tossing their caps into the air. No, I didn't say, 'Good-bye homeland.' I said, 'This isn't the same old joke, this is the start of something new; there's something behind this, and it's our job to keep our eye on it.' And what have I seen up to now?"

He looked around for something, an example of anything to turn his thoughts into words. He tore a leaf from the hedge of blackberry bushes behind him; it was like a little marjoram leaf in his big open palm. "If you prick yourself and you've got pus," he said, "you put this leaf on your wound and you'll see it drain it, pull out all the festering."

He asked me if I understood and I told him yes.

"That's how it was. Their laws or their regime or their examples pulled out what was festering in us, all the ugly things inside each of us, and it's so much better if they stay down underneath. We've seen a few righteous men acting on the same level as the most treacherous breed of greedy farmhands. And the disasters, the family squabbles and separations!"

Again I told him I understood. And he spread his arms again as if there were nothing else to say. But then he added, "Tomorrow? I don't know. After the festering maybe red blood comes. But I won't get to see it, that's for sure."

He pulled himself up. "What about the kolkhoz? Did it work here? No, it didn't. Everybody wants something all his own, be it large or small. They're going to put an end to it in October."

But here a tremendous fit of coughing came on him, and then another and a third and fourth, like the loud bursts of a machine gun. He went all red in the face and saliva sprayed from his mouth, and he stared at me with his little eyes, waving his hand.

"Mena!" he cried.

She came out calmly with a piece of cardboard, accustomed to it by now, and started fanning him below the nose, slowly, and patting him on the back. I wondered why she didn't shriek and call all the people of Giurizzani to come running with blankets, jackets, and overcoats to fan him below the nose.

"Light him a cigarette," she said. "No. One of his."

Then she went back into the house.

Again there was the stench of thorn apple, and soon Old Man Nin had his breath back.

A few more short bursts, and he took the cigarette from my hand and started to smoke it. "See?" he asked. "How can I tell you about tomorrow?"

He was back to smoking just as when I'd come.

"Go and find your happiness. It's left you here. You've got to chase it."

A big truck, loaded down as always, passed slowly along the road. The women came out onto the doorsteps and shaded their eyes with their hands. Auntie Mena came out too, and Old Man Nin raised his cane toward the truck.

"Who are they?" he asked loudly.

It was Margherita Ninelka who answered: "The Blosis from Cipiani."

I stood up. Old Man Nin said good-bye. The Blosis were coming in to say good-bye forever. He took up his pose, straightening the pencil behind his ear, puffing away and looking a little like a man past caring, but watching all the same from behind his glasses, to be ready, just in case, to put in a word or two.

■ □ ■ □ ■

XIII

IT WAS THE DAY BERTO AND I WERE PLOWING THE VINES IN Salía. The two- to three-week period during which you don't touch the bunches because they're liable to dry up had passed, and we could take animals along the rows because the grapes had started to ripen and were growing as flexible as rubber.

It had been a fine year. The fields were beautiful. The potatoes had come up well, the hay pretty well, the wheat really well, we'd dodged the hail, and now all we needed was two little inches of rain to strengthen the corn: then we'd have all we wanted.

But our field was located on a hill, and the land underneath was still wet. The two steers pulled like we were plowing in sand.

We finished an hour before sunset, and I'd taken the harness off the steers so they could graze where they liked along the paths.

Berto was sitting under the pear tree. I went up to him and offered him a cigarette.

We sat in silence, passing the flask with water and vinegar in it back and forth. Then we switched to the bottle of wine and started to talk.

"Well, Berto?"

"I don't know. You tell me, Franz."

"No. Now we're alone and we have to decide together. What do the women say?"

"You know them. They're like the others. They'd go at the drop of a hat, on foot even."

"And you?"

"I don't want to leave the land. We can't leave it, Francesco. It's ours and it's good land. None better anywhere."

"I agree. It's ours, but we can't have it. If we waited another ten years, things might sort themselves out. But what will be left of us and our kids in ten years? And what will be here in ten years?"

"So you're for going?"

"There's nothing else left. The way things are, we've no choice."

He propped himself up on his elbows and asked, "Even if they gave you the land?"

"Even if they gave me the land," I answered calmly.

He was chewing on a piece of grass and shaking his head, looking up. "Not me," he said. "I'd stay. I wouldn't give a damn about who's leaving or who's staying if I had my land."

I could feel him in my hands then. I could tell him what was welling up inside me. "Listen, Berto. I'm not the kind of guy to give lectures, but I want to tell you what I think. The land isn't everything, Berto. If it was, we'd have done everything to get it. But at a certain point we stopped. I gave it up the night Vanja and the others came to our place. We've got to think about our children, you and me. What kind of lesson would they learn if we stayed and entered the *skupčina* or I don't know what else? Old Man Nin was right: we're not made for this regime. Maybe it takes another kind of stomach. Or maybe you get used to it a little at a time, but I don't want that. I'm afraid of it. Didn't you see? They wanted me to sign that paper in order to disgrace a man. You're a lot younger. You don't think as much, and everything seems easy to you, so you almost fell for it. Even I barely recognized myself. We all have our self-interests and will do anything to defend them. Who's to say whether in ten years I wouldn't start swinging at you? Or go to the old man and take him by the throat and smack him in his hernia? And the children? Would you like your son to take you by the collar one day?"

Berto was taking me seriously. I was glad I had spoken.

A gust of the north wind came up from the sea, carrying the fragrance of freshly tilled soil, of red earth, the likes of which you can't find anywhere.

My brother took a deep breath, then lowered his head and said, "Let's go, Franz. We'll always be damned like the others. Let's leave now while the country's getting prettier by the day. Do you remember a year like this?"

"Yes. Twenty-two. You were little, you wouldn't remember."

"But doesn't it seem like fate?" he said. "All those years of frost or drought or hail, and now this. . . . Just look at the grapes!"

"It's on purpose. To make us strong, teach us how to choose and not let ourselves be tempted. It's like a warning from God. . . ."

"But shouldn't we get back at the bastard before we go and give him a nice little farewell party?"

"It's not worth it. He'll have misfortunes of his own come along, when he's alone like a dog. You can't eat land, can you? No, that man will bury himself."

It was dusk now, and the sun was floating into a pocket of clouds.

"Going to rain," said Berto. "The clouds are low over Salvore, and the sun's going in."

"There'll be enough for polenta."

We got to our feet, and I put a hand on his shoulder. "What are you afraid of, Berto? We're still together; our arms are still strong. We must never split up, no matter what happens. We've had some bad luck, but that's over now. The world's a big place. Agreed?"

"Agreed."

"So tomorrow morning I'm off to Umago."

It was evening by then, and the church bells were ringing, the Verteneglio and Carsette bells responding to the ones in

Buje, then ours in Materada, and those in Petrovia and San Lorenzo. As always, I carried the plow high to keep it from banging against the rocks, and Berto whistled, driving the animals forward.

That night I was awakened by thunder. Not that I would have slept much. I'd hardly dozed off and, on waking, was seized by my earlier thoughts. A barracks, I thought, two meals a day, milk in the morning, a small monthly subsidy. Elementary school for my daughter and a trade school for carpenters, mechanics, or bricklayers for Vigi. And then Australia, America, or Canada. Speaking a different language and eating and living differently. Or traveling around Italy and finding land to work. Farm workers again. There is good land there, even in Friuli. To yield enough corn and then some. But eventually I'd plant a few vines. What's a farm without vines? I could take along some malvasia grafts. Over there they train vines to climb the trunks. Our rows are better, slender and elegant like young ladies. You really enjoy the grape harvest. No, no one can beat us when it comes to vines. Each one needs something different, and we know how to work them and keep them going. Marco Zupan's nephew wrote that Istrian peasants are in great demand on Italian farms. So we find out what we need and get right to work. No waiting for manna from the heavens. Though we're not the first. Others have a head start. And if they bring up Uncle Matteo, we'll be back to square one.

There was a flash of lightning and a loud thunderclap. At the first splash of rain on the shades my wife woke up.

"Do you hear me, Francesco? What're you doing?"

"Thinking."

"You only think, never decide."

"But I have decided."

She turned to me and said, "Well?"

"I'm going to Umago tomorrow."

"Are you serious?"

"Ask Berto."

She nearly jumped on top of me. "And you didn't say anything to me?"

"You know now."

She wrapped both arms around my neck.

"I'm so happy, Francesco. For the children, you know. It's for them, Francesco. Here on the farm they'd always be poor—poor, ignorant servants. It's for them, believe me."

"I know," I said, listening to the big fat drops falling.

"It may even hail," she said, sticking her legs between mine. "Wouldn't you like a little hail to fall? You would, wouldn't you?"

"No, I wouldn't."

She was moving closer and closer, poking me and trying to look me in the face. "Really?"

"I said no."

"Not even on your uncle's fields?" she asked softly.

"Well, a few stones, but only there," I said by way of appeasement. She laughed. She was too close for me to let her go. When I finally did, there was a flash of lightning. Loud thunder followed, and Nita jumped up in her bed.

"Mama," she whimpered, "I'm afraid, Mama."

"Come here, silly. What are you afraid of?"

"The lightning. The flashes."

And she came over to us, looking like an angel in her long nightshirt. We put her between us as she wanted, and after a while, when she wanted to play, I said, "Would you like to go to Trieste?"

"When?"

"Soon."

"For long?"

"Forever. We're going there for good."

"Us too?"

"Us too."

"And the moo-cows?"

"We'll take the moo-cows with us."

"But is there a place for them to graze in Trieste?"

"We'll find a place."

"And will Uncle Matteo take them out to pasture?"

"We'll see. But you can take them."

"Sure I can. They know me now; they let me shepherd them. But there are lots of cars in Trieste. How can I take them out to pasture with all those cars?"

"We'll take them where there aren't any cars. And anyway, won't Fido be there to protect them?"

"But isn't it dangerous? He might bite somebody. Is it true there are lots of foreigners in Trieste?"

"Yes it is. But it's time to sleep now."

It wasn't long before she'd fallen back to sleep.

It had been a good rain. Good for the corn, I thought, and the grapes too. The bus was crowded as usual, and the radio was playing. The passengers were mostly office workers going to Umago, where the new regime had done great things: besides enlarging the Arrigoni factory, rebaptized as "Dragonja," it had built a dye factory, a pasta factory, a cement factory at Punta delle Vacche (which they claimed to be one of the biggest in Europe), a new wine shop, and the distilleries of Vino-Export. In Buje there were offices and prisons, and people took care of politics; in Umago they didn't waste any time and brought in the bricks—they worked. That's how all those new houses had sprung up, while the offices and prisons were no longer good for anything: they had gone back into the district of Pola.

For me Umago is the most beautiful place in the world: the sea flowing in between the two promontories, right up to the houses—there's nothing like it in the world. No wonder tourists have been flocking there from all over since they put up the new hotels. But while the heart and soul of the place used to be the pier, the church, and Mrs. Nina's hotel, it has now shifted to Punta, where the new hotels rise out of the woods and the rocks. Today the old town is completely abandoned. Everyone's left, as if they didn't care about the new town or knew it hadn't been built for them. Amidst those houses of another era, squeezed together around the bell tower, all you meet are cats and an occasional old man sunning himself and ready to tell you all about the winds and tides, and relate stories of bygone days. But you can't find a room there, not even for one night. Some leave; others come: Slovenes, Croats, Serbs, Bosnians, Montenegrins, and Dalmatians; in short, all the races gather in Umago to live and spend money like they've discovered America, they sleep on top of one another—good for anyone who understands something in all this—and once in a while you hear that two of them have gone at it with knives and a woman has drowned herself after.

The line at town hall came down the steps and all the way out to the gate; and everyone in it was waiting to appear before the windows of the emigration office. But things were moving along fast, and people were pushing their way up the stairs. They were from Giubba and Salvore, from Seghetto, Gezzi, and Madonna del Carso. From our parts I saw only Mario Farletta, from Grotta, though he hadn't seen me yet. He was in front of me, his head down and his neck gleaming with sweat. It didn't take long for me to sweat, too.

At first it seemed easy, but as I got closer to the windows, my legs started shaking and my throat grew dry; I would have given anything for a glass of beer.

A bed, two meals, a subsidy—I was thinking—and land. And harvesting the wheat and picking the grapes and having the money in my pocket by St. Martin's Day, and then you can go to Gelmo's for a hand of cards. And then the Christmas holidays, you butcher a pig, New Year's, a little money for the kids, Heaven help you if a woman comes in first, Epiphany, stockings above the fireplace, hoeing and plowing, wagonloads of steaming manure, then covered with frost, carnival, a hunchback made out of hay and a couple of charcoal mustache smudges and a giant frittata with eggs and sausages collected from house to house, Easter. And the hay, a red handful of clover in an empty steer horn, and you're eating outside amidst sweet fragrances, alfalfa, red potatoes in red soil, wheat and threshing, holidays again, on and on in the same way, until you can buy yourself something new, build yourself a barn, repair the bread oven, mend the roof, plant new vines.

Now I was on the stairs too.

And buying my wife a dress, seeing my daughter cooking with a scarf in her hair, making bread, Vigi with a girlfriend who comes to the house. Going together to a fair, with a little carriage and maybe a small horse like Nando's, coming home with a melon, everyone a little tired. Going to the beach in summer with umbrellas.

"You too, friend?" asked Farletta, turning around.

"Yeah, me too."

I stood with my head down. He too was staring at the glossy stone steps worn down by a finger-breadth in just these few months. "The women asked me to buy yeast," he said. "Think I'll have time? When do the shops close?"

"I don't know. Wait, the shops you said? Let me see. At about . . . No, I don't know."

And having a good friend, who understands you—I thought. There are things you can't say to your wife or brother or son. A friend. Having him come over for lunch, and then going to his place. Because I've never had friends, people who listen to me, think about me, watch over me; people I give things, bits of my heart, you might say.

"There's a bus before noon. Will we be able to take care of it all by then? And buy the yeast?"

"Wait. They're on the summer schedule, and the bus. . . . No, I don't know."

What kind of a girl will my son end up with? He's so quiet. Long legs. But what kind of guy is he? Will he know how to act with women? Now he'll have to find a girl over there. And then children. My son with children? Now Nita's the kind of girl who'll tease all the toughs until the right one comes along, and then keep your eye on her. The same old story, of course.

"Your turn, friend."

"No. You got here first. Don't be silly. I saw you."

"No, you go first."

"What do you mean? Go on, be brave. It'll be over in no time. You can wait for me at the bus, and I'll run and buy the yeast."

And having a snack on the grass. Taking stock of my life. Then there's my uncle. Bastard. Thief. And Franjo. Two-faced. And the rest of them. The slap. But there were two. And the second was harder. Thieves. They're all the same. Look at the clerks they've got. So this is civilization.

"Name?"

"Francesco Koslović."

"Father's name."

"Giovanni."

"Mother's?"

"Maria Trento."

"Birthdate?"

"July 26, 1912."

"You have a brother?"

"I have."

"Is he going too?"

"He is too."

"Sign here. And here below for him."

I turned to see Mario Farletta giving someone else his place. "See you at the bus, friend, at the bus."

I went down the steps and headed straight for the nearest beer.

But I made the trip on foot—there was no time to lose—and reached Milio's house just when they were having lunch under the arbor.

"Hello."

"Hello."

"*Buon appetito.*"

"Thanks."

"How're you?"

"Fine. And you?"

"Fine. I've just been to Umago."

"To get yourself some yeast?"

I laugh and, laughing, say, "To get myself some yeast."

He puts down his spoon. Studies me.

"It will make the women happy."

"You can bet on it."

Then they all sat there staring at me. Milio's son Bruno asked me how come.

"I just did it, that's all. It's in the air. Bye."

"Wait. Want to have lunch with us?"

"No thanks. I've got dinner waiting for me at home."

They were all at the door when I pushed open the cane gate, and Uncle Matteo was spying through the blinds. They waited motionless, and I let them wait while I removed the mud from my shoes. But Nita came up with her hand out, asking for candy. "I haven't got any, Nita. Forgive me. There was no time."

We all looked at one another. "How did it go?" asked Berto.

"As expected."

There was a silence, a long silence. Then my wife burst into tears and rested her cheek on my sister-in-law's shoulder. My uncle closed the blinds, and she turned and faced upward and no longer looked like herself. I don't know if she was cursing him or God. Screaming with rage, she soon reached the point when you leap out of your normal state, when neither father nor mother nor husband nor children exist, when there is only the smell of salt and the pain in your head and tears swollen and glittering like stars. That's what happened to my wife. She screamed at the top of her lungs and shook her fists, red in the face, while Maria held her back. "Coward, cheat! It's all your fault we have to go wandering like beggars! Thief, thief! You stole that land! From your own nephews, your flesh and blood. How can you look people in the face? But now your time's up, so eat your land

and then rot under the rocks! Eat it, eat it, what are you waiting for? And then I hope it comes out of your ears and your eyes and you burst like a worm! Never a kind word, just orders, tricks, and rudeness, ever since I came to this damn mountain!"

Her words infected my sister-in-law too. She had let her go and was screaming herself. And then Berto too, and my son. All four were screaming and crying, and Berto was blaspheming the Lord and the Virgin Mary.

I was too tired. I sat down on a rock and let them do as they pleased.

XIV

THE NEXT MORNING I HITCHED UP THE WAGON, SPREAD TWO pitchforks of straw in the bottom, and loaded the large barrel. The old man had seen me pouring the wine but didn't dare ask any questions and soon disappeared behind the gate.

Berto came with me to Giurizzani. But it wasn't like with the calf; now the situation was reversed. Uncle Matteo was waiting for me in front of the cooperative, and he had Franjo with him. They watched us coming like innocent bystanders. Seeing them next to each other, I realized in a way I never had before that Franjo was his nephew too, they were one of a kind.

I didn't greet them; I didn't say anything until Giovanni Bože came. He was in charge of purchasing wine for the cooperative and the one I had to deal with.

"It's full, Giovanni. There's just under a hundred and ninety gallons."

"Good," he said. "Did you weigh the empty barrel?"

"No, we'll weigh it afterward."

My uncle glanced at Franjo. "I know, Giovanni," he said. "You think I don't know my own equipment? Empty it weighs exactly one hundred and eighty-five pounds."

"We'll weigh it afterward, Giovanni," I said.

Berto and I carried the keg to the scale and then emptied it into one of the big casks belonging to the *zadruga*. The old man came up behind me to check the weight, then looked over at Franjo as if they were agreeing about something.

"Look what fine nephews you've got, Uncle Matteo," Franjo said. "Doing everything themselves. Don't want you to have to lift a finger."

I didn't respond: I knew he wanted to provoke me. I just said to Giovanni, "Didn't I tell you it was just under a hundred and ninety?"

"Shall I write up the receipt now?" he asked.

"I'll come back. I'm in no hurry."

"But I am," my uncle butted in. "I want it now."

Giovanni looked over at Uncle Matteo, but Franjo intervened: "Write it up for him. He's in a hurry."

"What's going on here?" I said, flaring up.

"Nothing," said my uncle. "I've sold my wine, and I want a receipt."

"If that's the way you want it . . . Giovanni, give me the receipt right now."

But Franjo came up almost on top of me and said, "Receipt for what?"

"I'm not discussing it with you. You don't count. What business is it of yours anyway?"

"No, what business is it of *yours?* Aren't you going to Trieste? Well, what are you waiting for? What are you doing here?"

I turned back to Giovanni and said, "You're the one I'm dealing with here. Are you going to write me a receipt?"

Giovanni took out his notepad and pencil. But the old man went up to his back and said, "What are you doing? Are you crazy or something? Whose name are you writing?"

"His name. He brought me the wine. The money goes to him."

"But that's stealing, taking what's somebody else's."

"That's of no interest to me. He brought it, he unloaded it."

"Yeah, it's stealing," said Franjo.

"Then turn him in," he said and started writing.

Neither suspected that Giovanni would resist them. There was a short silence, and then the old man grumbled to Franjo, "Are you going to stand by and watch them rob me?"

At that Franjo shouted, "You watch your step, Giovanni. You going to listen to me or not?"

"You watch your step, Franjo. Be reasonable for once. I know what I'm doing."

"But the wine is his."

"That's what you say. But who worked the vines? Your uncle sold seven hundred gallons in February. Isn't that enough for him? That time I made out the receipt in his name; today's different."

"Because they're going to Italy and he's staying here and joining the *skupčina* with us?"

Giovanni nearly lost his temper. "I'd like to tell you a thing or two if we were alone, but now I'll just say watch your step."

"So they can take anything they like and pocket the money? I've never seen such lawlessness in my life!"

Since Giovanni didn't have a comeback, I jumped in and said, "That's right. I'm selling the animals too or taking them together with some other things. I've decided not to talk to you, Uncle Matteo, unless there are witnesses, so this is a good time to let you know that Berto and I are going to keep working the land until we leave because we can't stand around with our hands in our pockets. And you'll harvest it all. But what we're taking we're taking. If you have any problem with that, let's go and see the judge. I'm leaving you the land; I wouldn't know what to do with it since now it's cursed. But I claim the right to sell what I've grown and make back some of what you got fat on all those years. I'm speaking as a worker, which is what I've always been, and that means blood, sweat, and tears, or whatever you want to call it."

The two of them left, grumbling that that wouldn't be the end of it, and while their stench was in the air, I said, "Look, Giovanni. I have an idea. Maybe it's nothing, but I'm going to tell it to you before it gets away. There are two kinds of men. Honest and dishonest. When we were unloading the wine and I saw those two calmly waiting to step up and make their claims, I thought, that's what some of the workers did in '45 and that's what the bosses always did once. But the day I harvested the wheat I could have easily waited until my uncle's workers had cut it and then come when it was all ready and taken it home with me. But no. I felt it was mine and so cut it myself, cut it as far as I felt it belonged to me. I don't know if I'm making sense, Giovanni, but there are two kinds of men and two ways of giving orders and making claims. And only one right and holy way to keep your head high. And I think it depends on a person's character. But I'm all mixed up; maybe I didn't explain it how I wanted."

"There you are," he said, tearing off the receipt and smiling. "Stop in and say good-bye before you leave."

Outside Milio was talking to Berto in front of the animals. He waved when he saw me and said, "Just the guy I was looking for."

He'd had a little to drink and sounded like a woman.

"The truck has come. I need men to load it. You know how it is. After helping all the others, I've got nobody to help me. That's how it'll be for you when it's your turn. Sorry I won't be able to help you, but you'll be paid back another day. So are you coming or are you sending your brother? It won't take but half an hour."

"I'll come," I said.

"Did you sell the wine?" he asked on the way. "Good for you. It might've turned to vinegar if you'd waited."

Milio—wouldn't you know it—had all sorts of good-for-nothing trifles: planes, saws, hammers, trowels, and hoes, plus a gigantic chest that took up a lot of space. He was one of the few peasant-farmers in our parts who planted and cultivated everything in small quantities: fruit trees, chicory, strawberries, peas. He had pigeon boxes along the front part of the house, a small beehive, and cages of rabbits in the barn together with the steers. He had more than a thousand pounds of walnuts, almonds, hazelnuts, watermelons, cantaloupes, and August grapes to load. It was his art, you might say; his fields looked like gardens.

Before anyone got on the truck, the Serb customs official would inspect it. Milio paid no attention to that and climbed onto it like a cat. But the official ordered him down and had him take everything out of his pockets. And Milio, looking straight at him and laughing with the small shiny eyes in his little weasel-like face, dropped to the ground, piece by piece, his handkerchief, his comb, a ball of string, his pocketknife, and tin of tobacco.

Then he asked, "*Hoćete li i cipele?*" (You want the shoes too?)

The official stared at him hard.

"*I cipele.*" (The shoes too.)

And Milio slowly removed one worn-out shoe and sock and stretched out a naked white foot, slightly stained with the red earth that gets in everywhere.

"*Dosta!*" (Enough!) said the Serb, and Milio climbed back onto the truck. But it took all the patience in the world to help him. First he shouted for the chest, then no, the sacks, then no again: the first thing he wanted to put in was his old stove and the disassembled bed.

His wife, Stefania, always took him seriously, but his two sons snickered and winked at me to let me know he'd had a bit to drink. But here, too, he stowed everything in order, making use of the smallest spaces. We lost time because the customs man was suspicious (he refused even a glass of wine and a slice of watermelon) and checked every piece, weighing the potatoes and wheat to the last pound and wanting to peer into the cracks of the Madonna over the bed in order to look inside the cracks. "But what do you expect to find?" Milio asked, making matters worse.

When the truck was all loaded, we sat down under the arbor to have lunch. His wife had had help from two women who were staying in Giurizzani and were doing well now that the town was almost abandoned. They'd prepared gnocchi with dove meat, and seeing them bustle around the house in their kerchiefs and all made it seem like a wedding day or fair or baptism. Meanwhile, Milio was wondering how to get back at the customs man and vent his bile. He invited the truck driver to the table; he invited me. His sons came and sat down. "*Buon appetito*," he said, attacking his plate of gnocchi and then pouring our drinks.

It was very hot, and the Serb official stood by, looking at us silently, blankly, in a world of his own. Then he went under the quince tree and took out his satchel. He unwrapped his lunch: it was black bread and a piece of lard. He started eating slowly, still looking at us with that blank look of his. When he'd eaten his fill, he put the leftovers back in his satchel and wiped his hands and chin. "*Sad idemo*," he said. "*Žuri mi se*" (Let's go; I'm in a hurry).

The driver dropped everything and was in the truck in a flash.

Milio protested. There was some commotion, some running here and there. His sons convinced him it was better to keep quiet. One of the women collected everything on the plates in a big pot: a feast for her. The house was emptied of all the little things that had been used for lunch. They dressed in a hurry and said their good-byes. The usual tears and twisted faces.

Even Milio's face was contorted like that of a boy who's just been slapped and mustn't show it. And he didn't. He turned to the people and the half-finished lunch and said, "There's the last of their brave deeds!"

Then he let down the blinds, locked the door, and, assuming an important air, was about to toss the key into the hollow of the limekiln, where there was always some standing water, but his wife took it out of his hand and tucked it into her bosom.

"Good-bye, Milio," I said. "Good luck. See you over there."

I walked behind the truck for a while, and seeing the space left in the rear, I thought it too big to have entered Milio's little realm and emerged an hour later taking everything with it.

The two youngsters had jumped on top while Milio and Stefania waited on some rocks in front of the house for the car coming from Umago.

■ □ ■ □ ■

X V

THAT YEAR THE FAIR FELL ON A TUESDAY, SO THERE WERE three holidays: Sunday; Monday, which was considered a half-holiday; and the fair itself, of the Virgin of the Snow, which comes on the fifth of August.

Sunday evening Berto and I waited till the women had put the children to bed, and all four of us went down to Giurizzani together.

There was no light, and the town—between the people who'd left, the empty houses, and the darkness—seemed abandoned to a continual night.

Even the season was different; instead of crickets in the shrubs, you heard owls beating their death signals from the rooftops.

There was a little group waiting motionless at the aqueduct. When we got closer, we saw it was Sandro Bonazza and his wife, Femia, arm in arm with their daughter.

"I knew there was still somebody who wanted to celebrate," said Sandro.

"How come even the capital is dark tonight?"

"It's the last dance. They didn't want us to get too tired."

"A few more days and we'd have to carry lanterns," said Berto.

"Still, the dance is on," said Femia.

"Your feet are always itching to dance."

"It's a sign I feel young and strong."

"Let's go if you promise me the first round."

"The first two for you, Franz. As long as your wife doesn't drag me away by the hair."

"Be my guest, but you'll see soon enough he's forgotten how to move his feet."

The men came to a stop in front of Gelmo's. "Maybe we'll get a beer," I said. "Would you like an orange drink?" But the women had heard the band. "Wait for us there then and get a table."

"You hurry up though," Femia responded quickly, like a young girl.

"Who're you so eager to see?" I asked.

"You."

"Me and Berto?"

"You mostly!" she said, taking Maria and my wife by the arm, and, laughing, they set off for the Dom.

We suddenly seemed young again—sending the girls ahead and going to the tavern and making a ruckus, and not because you really wanted to drink. Just going into Gelmo's was enough to make you young again.

There were only a few people inside. Two of them, at a table, I didn't recognize. Rozzan was standing at the counter, talking to Italo, who had an air of leaving about him. But it was Gelmo who was the most pitiful. Everybody knew he had been arguing with his wife about whether to leave. First, he was the one who wanted "to pack up and get out," and she swore if he did he'd die in the trousers he had on; then she started whispering in his ear it was going to be like in Russia here, with everything collectivized, and now he swore that nothing on earth would make him leave his own hard work to others. In short, they were at loggerheads. And lately he went around in tattered clothes to make people feel sorry for him. He wanted others to decide for him or at least to forgive him for whatever decision he made.

Now he was sitting at a table looking like an old beggar who has scraped together the money for a glass of wine.

"So, Gelmo, how're things?" asked Sandro.

Gelmo gave him a sour look and, as if continuing a conversation, waved his hand slowly and said, "Here today, gone tomorrow. What's all the fuss about?"

"Not too many people here tonight, Gelmo," said Berto, jokingly. "What's going on?"

Again he waved his hand and said, as if to himself, "What's the fuss? For the three or four days we've got left in the world. Here today, gone tomorrow."

Rozzan gave a wink as if to say he could tell what Gelmo's words meant. He clearly felt like talking to me but lacked the courage to look me in the face. It was painful to see. Like on that evening of the conference. "People aren't sleeping these days," he said. But nobody responded.

"Know anyone who is?" he asked, polishing the zinc counter.

Silence. He glanced over at the two strangers sitting at the table talking. Then he turned to me and asked, "How about you? You sleeping?"

His eyes were red, like Milio's on that distant evening, in this same bar. "Sure I am," I said. "The air's fresh up at our place, and there aren't any mosquitoes."

I had answered, and that was all he needed. He was at my back, speaking softly, breathlessly. "They're already here. See them? Sitting at that table, with the long hair. From the hinterland, the mountains, to see their new home. They'll have their pick of houses. They've been living in chicken coops like animals, and now they may even take Nando's place."

"They're right," I said. "It's only fair."

I remembered Femia, paid for the beers, and pushed the others in the direction of the Dom, the women, and the fair.

The dance was in the open, on a cement floor laid not long before. The band was half its usual size. With Milio's sons gone, and Renato and Gualtiero, they were missing the clarinets and the trumpet and bass. Fioravante was doing what he could with the baritone and he had invited Giona to give him a hand with his old harmonica. That was why they were playing only polkas and mazurkas and older songs.

There weren't many people: some youngsters clamoring like they'd been left behind and were trying to catch up, and a group of boys standing around drinking.

The women were waiting for us at a table and said we'd been as good as our word.

Giovanni Bože passed by, patting me on the back; he looked like a different man. Even he had got what he wanted. A few days before, the officer from Petrovia had sneaked off and everybody had been saying he'd left Giovanni's daughter pregnant. But now Femia said, "He didn't deserve that. He's a good man; he did what he could. Besides, when people are young . . ."—she seemed to be talking just to me; I kept the joke going—". . . you want to do everything your own way." And she countered, "Or else you believe everything you hear right off."

By then Giovanni had jumped up onto the platform where the band was and the carbide lamp, and said in a cheerful tone, "And now a turn for the emigrants! All emigrants out on the floor!"

The band started playing and nearly everyone got up. I took Femia by the arm, told her that this was our dance, and we started to polka.

"There are a lot of people emigrating," she said, looking around and nodding in the direction of Franjo's son (the one who'd become a teacher after barely two years of study), who was dancing with a girl from Petrovia. "Any girl will make you lose your head, and that one's from Petrovia. Everyone from there is leaving. And the girls from Petrovia have always had what it takes."

I pulled her close and noticed she smelled of powder and must be very clean underneath. I started losing my head with this sweetheart from once upon a time, with the dance and the carbide lamp from once upon a time. "The polkas we danced, Femia," I said. "Where was it you lost that shoe?"

"At the Gambozzi dance, on the plank floor outside. But it was a joke, I never told you. A guy from Vinella gave me a push and another guy took it away from me in secret."

"You were always surrounded by men. They followed you around. Remember the night they started throwing stones at you and you had me called from the bar?"

"That time it was girls. There was one from Petrovia. They were jealous, always after me."

"Afraid for their boyfriends."

"They were the ones who followed me around."

"And you didn't do anything to deserve it?"

She gave me a little push and said, "You've got some nerve. You know who I wanted for my one and only."

I knew it wasn't true, but since that was how the evening was going, I almost believed her and it made me happy. She let me hold her a little tighter, and I felt her powder taking hold, and her still-youthful flesh, and her dark complexion, and the memory of the haystacks where she rubbed against me in ways I can't describe. But she immediately slipped free and said, "Let's dance normal, or your wife will get upset." Then, looking straight into my eyes, she added, "And for no reason."

It was that more than anything that made me lose my head.

We went back to the table. The boys were all worked up. They had decided to make their own contribution, and now, sitting at a table, pounding their glasses and laughing, they were calling for drinks. Then one got to his feet, told the others to be quiet, and led them all in the following:

Just four days more,
And we'll be off,
Materada youth
Will all be gone.

"Well done!" shouted Femia, clapping. "Listen to that, will you!"

But people hushed her, as if they were at mass, and a few of them shouted, "Encore! Encore! Sing it again!"

But Riccardo's son said you can't sing without lining the throat, so somebody bought them a liter, somebody else a double liter, and somebody else yet another liter "for those fine boys of ours." Giovanni Bože called out, "Take it easy. They're young. It'll go right to their heads," but everybody just thought he was afraid of the police, and they shouted and pounded on the tables that they wanted to hear them sing—why not, what was so terrible?

By now there seemed to be fifty or sixty of them.

Just four days more,
And we'll be off,
Materada youth
Will all be gone.

I thought of my son, who I didn't see among them. He must have gone to see the girl from Castelvenere he'd been dancing with three Sundays running.

I found the song painful. It used to be sung when men went into the army. You didn't think about the words, you just sang and were rowdy, as if the words had been invented for somebody else or just to go with the music. But now I heard only the words, and I thought what was a town without its young people and what would those raw youths be without the town whose air they'd breathed and bread they'd eaten. Even I felt I was leaving behind my youth, scattered a little here, a little there, in a hedge, behind a pile of straw, in the air, at the foot of one of the countless little walls dividing our fields. And I looked at Femia.

I'd been dancing only with my wife so she wouldn't have anything to be suspicious about. But Femia didn't understand, and after an hour or so, thinking I was offended or giving her the cold shoulder, she touched me under the table, pushed me with her knee, and leaned against me with her thigh, while talking loudly and laughing with the others. I responded by saying I was really hot. She laughed.

Those poor boys couldn't in fact hold the wine. They were no longer happy with singing; they wanted to raise Cain. They were standing, clinking glasses, and spilling wine all over themselves. But hardly anybody noticed. They were struggling with themselves or with the wine in their own stomachs.

I danced again with my wife. I saw Berto telling Sandro the whole story of my uncle and didn't stop him. When the dance was over, I went up to Sandro and said, "I need some sacks for wheat and potatoes. You wouldn't have any you could lend me, would you?"

Femia held her breath.

Sure he had. Sacks and anything else I might need. Thank God, he'd always had enough of everything.

Femia still wasn't breathing.

"Well," I said, "could your daughter run and get them?"

Femia relaxed her grip a little. But his daughter made a wry face. To go home at night in the dark, and during the last dance!

"Well, Sandro, what do you say?" But he was a gentleman; he was sipping his glass of wine with his little finger in the air: I could go if I wanted, take the whole house, he wouldn't care.

Femia jumped up and said, a little angrily, "All right then, I'll go."

And to appease her I shrugged and ran after her, saying I'd keep her company, and I heard my wife say, "I trust you two!" behind me.

The boys were singing again, out of tune, "All be gone! All be gone!"

In the dark, on the road, we felt alone, the two of us, and united by the trick we'd played on everybody. Passing Gelmo's she said, "Let's go this way. Somebody might see us."

I felt shy like a schoolboy, and all I could say was, "Don't worry, Femia. Who could see us now?"

But it wasn't easy. My legs were shaking. There I was in her kitchen, while she pretended to look for those sacks and I lit matches for her and held them until they burned my fingers.

She was more resolute and said, "Maybe they're in the dining room. Light the way for me." There we found two wet sacks filled with wool and others still empty and dry.

"I emptied the mattresses," she said, "to wash the wool."

We stood there a moment in silence. She picked up the dry sacks I'd asked her husband for. There was no more reason to stay, I could take up the sacks and leave. But I said, my voice shaking, "Femia, why was it when I came back from the army you didn't want to see me?"

I could feel she'd been waiting for that question, and she was ready to answer. "I never told you," she said, furious, "but your mother was not a nice woman. Or fair. And what she wrote you in the letter wasn't true. How could she say I betrayed you? I wasn't with anybody else, I swear. She made it up. It was all her own scheming. And why? Because I was poor, I didn't have acres of land or cows or gold to take her as a dowry! That's why and only that! And what have you got now? You're poor: no land, no house; you're on the street like me!"

Her whole body shook as she spoke. She gasped for breath. I stood there with my mouth open and thought the wine had gone to her head too. I took two steps forward, grabbed her firmly by the waist, and said into the dark, "What are you saying? Why are you bringing that up now? I don't want to hear any of it, understand? It's ancient history. I don't want to hear it."

But she didn't let me finish. She slipped out of my grasp and went on breathlessly, "She thought the Koslovićes would rule over all Materada one day. I wasn't made for your kind. I was poor. I just had one goat to send out to pasture. No steers, no cows. She needed somebody else, somebody with goods and property. And who did you come up with? Somebody like me. She's a good woman, I know. But what did she have that I didn't have? What kind of a dowry did she bring you?"

I grabbed her again and squeezed her hard, covering her mouth with my hand. I nearly gave her a slap.

She managed to get away and was even more enraged. "But there's a God," she said. "You don't know how much I suffered. At first I went limp, but then I realized you weren't any better than your mother and you didn't deserve me, even if I had no steers or land. You wanted them too, you didn't care about anything else. I was too poor for you. But there's a God, like I said."

"What are you talking about?" I shouted, all but choking. "How can you say those things? Did you see me at a dance or a party for the whole year after I came back from the army? I didn't know, Femia. Everyone had something to tell me about you, not just my poor mother. So now you wish me ill? You're happy I've been treated badly and like you I'm on the street?"

We heard the steps of people walking in the direction of Cipiani and, farther off, an indistinct song coming closer.

Femia was breathing heavily. I felt that she was sorry for saying what she'd said and that she'd said it only because of the state we were all in. I felt terrible.

By now we could hear the words of the song. It was two boys returning home from the dance, and they sang,

> The train is parting, so is the steamer,
> And so too is my very first,
> My very first love,
> And so too is my very first. . . .

She rushed up and threw her arms around my neck and begged me to forgive her. She bathed my face in her tears.

A second group was passing, and now the voices were strong, the words clear. They seemed to be singing for me and Femia.

> And so too is my very first,
> My very first love,
> And so too is my very first. . . .

She was a little thing, trembling and crying, and it was strange that the war or the Liberation or an agreement among ministers had affected the little thing I held in my arms, had pierced the little heart pounding next to mine.

Weeping, Femia said, "What happened to us, Cesco? And what will happen now? Everything's ready. It's any day now. I sold my radio today. The nice radio I whiled away the hours with. You could hear it all the way to Petrovia. Who'll enjoy my nice radio now?"

She sobbed, and her narrow life trembled under my hands, and I tried to calm her and dried her tears, and said, "It's nothing, Femia. We can still put the world in order. Everything can go back to how it was before for us poor things."

"Not how it was before, Francesco. Don't say how it was before."

Again I felt her powder go to my head, and her still-youthful flesh—her carefree nature and total readiness for lovemaking—and the memory of our haystacks.

We could hear the song in the distance:

My very first love
And so too is my very first. . . .

Slowly she let herself down onto those two sacks of wet wool and, experienced as she was, laid the dry ones I held in my hand on top. And by the little of the moon coming into the room, I saw her in that pose that to her might have been natural but that I had always considered ours alone. And so, I took that evening, again and for always, the little bit that remained in her of me and gave to her the bit that remained in me of her. And when she got up, slightly sheepish, I reached out almost as if to brush the hay from her hair.

"Those times are gone, Francesco," she said. "Maybe I've made a fool of myself."

"No," I said. "The years don't seem to pass for you."

And before going out, I glanced at the sacks that had welcomed us for the last time, the sacks containing the wool from her mattresses.

In the street we could hear that the song wasn't dead at all. But the voices were hoarse, as if mixed with the scirocco.

My very first love
And so too is my very first. . . .

"You go this way," I said. "I'll come after you."

"No, they might get suspicious. It's better to go back together."

"Okay, then wait for me up ahead. I'll be right there."

"What about the sacks?"

I dissolved into voiceless laughter. Joining in, she said, "I'll go and get them and wait for you at Gelmo's."

I listened to her quick steps moving away. I couldn't make out the song anymore, but now it was lodged in my head and wouldn't stop singing to me:

My very first love
And so too is my very first. . . .

I went down to the aqueduct to wash my hands.

■ □ ■ □ ■

X V I

THE FAIR TOOK PLACE TWO DAYS LATER. NO MASS, NO DANCE, but the few people left still wanted to celebrate it. Oliva had killed a hen, Maria was helping her pluck its feathers under the oak, and Berto and I were making crates for the departure. We would have had our own family celebration and then maybe gone to Gelmo's in the evening, but suddenly the church bell started chiming.

We broke off work and looked at one another.

"Didn't they say they weren't going to have mass?" Maria said.

"They did," said Oliva. "There's no priest to come say it."

"But the bell's ringing. What could be happening in Materada?"

"It's the August Virgin. What else could it be? They're ringing to bless the fields."

"No, it's something else," said Maria. "Maybe that Croatian priest has come from Buje."

"You're joking. You think a Croat's going to come here to say mass?"

"They're certainly calling people to mass."

"It's been ringing a long time. Like for All Souls' Eve."

"Oliva, you take care of lunch. I'll run and see."

"I'm coming too," I said. And twenty minutes later we were in Materada.

The few men I found at the bell tower were all elderly. They didn't know any more than I did about what was going on. They were simply standing around in their black jackets and their collarless shirts, asking one another if anybody had seen the priest.

"It might be the Buje priest," said a man from Sferchi, "but where's his motorbike?"

"Besides, the sacristy is locked. And where are Marco Zupan, Nini Pellegrin, and the other church board members? And Bortolo Mustacchia? Why aren't they here?"

"What we need to find out is who rang the bells."

"They may have left already."

"No, they haven't," said a boy. "I saw Nini Pellegrin going into the sacristy from the cemetery door."

Women were greeting one another, going into the church. The group of men had grown. There were youngsters from Sferchi and Cipiani. Everybody was asking questions, everybody wanted to find out what was up. Bortolo's son came out of the church, but he only smiled and said, "Go on in; I'm just going to give the last bell strokes."

We sat down in the pews. Marco Zupan came out of the sacristy and lit the candles with a long rod. The outside bell stopped ringing, and the little one next to the altar started instead. Everyone stared at the little door of the sacristy, and when it opened, out came six altar boys and Bortolo Mustacchia, book in hand. He had always loved church affairs: he sang for all the funerals and during Holy Week, helped the sexton with the important masses, and there wasn't a pastoral luncheon in our district he didn't attend.

And here he was first kneeling at the altar in the middle of the altar boys, then coming up to the balustrade. He put on his glasses, fastening them with a string behind his ears, and began to talk.

It took all his courage, because with the exception of the parish priest, no one had ever spoken directly to the people sitting in the pews. But he found the courage, and, small and heavy and red in the face as he was, smoothing his drooping mustache, he said, "My friends. Today is our fair. Today is the Virgin of the Snow, the holy protector of Materada. Is it not right to celebrate it as in years past? Indeed, this year we need to pray to her more than in any other year. Because today we're still here together—only a few of us, but still together—and tomorrow where will we be and what will have become of all of us? So don't expect a priest. No priest has come. This morning I recalled the beautiful fairs we used to have, when not one but six priests would come, and we had three bells chiming, celebrating with us and ringing out, and I thought of all of you at home, dressed up, waiting, and so I started ringing the bell. Marco Zupan and Nini Pellegrin and the others, who are good men and who have always done their bit for our church, they agree with me. There won't be any priest, but we'll say mass all the same. We're the ones who say it anyway. And after, if you want, we'll make the tour around the cemetery."

The altar boys sat down on the altar steps, and Bortolo went over to the cantor's bench and started singing the Kyrie. They all followed him, as best they knew how.

I've never been good at that sort of thing, but I sang too, behind the youngsters from Sferchi; and I thought of the masses when you could barely see the priests for the incense, and Nino Bonetti would play the harmonium, and a baby would babble loudly, while the bells sounded outside where there was an ice cream vendor, and what with all those people in the little church, a woman would feel faint and have to be helped out by two men to a bench in the fresh air.

After the Kyrie we sang the Gloria. The Fernettich brothers had put on their slippers and moved over to the cantor's bench. They looked resuscitated from a long illness. They all read the Latin without thinking and would constantly steal glances at the priest, afraid they had let slip a curse, but now they were free, masters of the situation (who understood Latin anyway?), and they sang in mutual harmony, making the most of what was left of their strong, "church" voices given the wine and tobacco buried in their throats.

Halfway through the Credo, without any signal, we rose to our feet. Marco Zupan had taken the banner of San Rocco and given it to one of the boys from Sferchi. Another took the processional cross, a third took a large funeral candle. In silence, someone took up another banner, someone else a lantern. People seemed ready to turn the church inside out, but in a careful, orderly manner. The singing continued. I found an old paneless lantern in my hands. There wasn't a person who wasn't carrying one such implement.

We left the church for the cemetery a few steps away. It was noon, and the bell started chiming again. We were singing the Credo, and now our song floated out over the low stone wall and down to the fields below. You could hear the bells of Buje, then those of Carsette, and Verteneglio, Petrovia, and San Lorenzo.

The weeds in the cemetery were tall and dry; they covered the tombs. The women had struck up the song to the Virgin: "We are sinners but your children." And I thought how useless the words were now, how out of place, that it was just the singing that mattered.

The other bells fell silent; only ours resisted. But then it, too, seemed ready to stop and, after a few loud chimes, died completely. The singing stopped as well.

Suddenly we felt the heat and heard the steps of the women shuffling in the weeds.

I looked at the tombs. What with all their weeds they looked like mounds of earth on the backs of enormous moles. And I thought of our deceased, their ears and nostrils filled with sweet basil; I thought of so many other people who'd been born and bred and then buried there with a rosary and a black book in their hands, and of whom nothing was left but bones and more bones, the ones on top of the others, and books and beads strewn through the soil. An acre of that rockless land had sufficed for them all; it could have sufficed for us and our children too.

"Farewell to our dead," said one woman aloud.

■ □ ■ □ ■

WRITINGS FROM AN UNBOUND EUROPE